I0549492

Crack the Spine
Fall 2013

Edited by Kerri Farrell Foley

This anthology is generously sponsored by Outskirts Press

Collection Copyright © 2013 Crack the Spine Press, LLC.

Individual works are the sole property of the authors.

ISBN-10: 0988978245
ISBN-13: 978-0-9889782-4-9

Library of Congress Control Number 2013920780

Published by Crack the Spine Press, LLC.
Printed in the United States of America.

Crack the Spine Press, LLC
Houston, Texas
Hattiesburg, Mississippi
www.crackthespinepress.com

CONTENTS

Eating Madame Bovary

Pets the cover   with the back
  of his hand, fingernails lingering   on her face,
   as if caressing   a live cheek
    title page: MADAME BOVARY   centered in all-caps

Swirls
of ink envelop the name   in flowers
He inhales   for six seconds
Hold   for four
Out   for six

Opens the drawer,   pulls out
scissors   blows to clean,
cut once into   spine

Six in.
   Four.
Six out.

Six.
   Four.
Six.

   Cut again, page on top of the rest   loose, naked
  the page to the light,   a cashier with a
  $100 bill   Light mottled through yellow-grey paper
His eyes follow the swirls

                the way he would follow Emma's
   curves   Paper to his nose and lips

1

dusty perfume   groping erect

nose hairs, traveling to his skull   his lips on the page,
top one on MADAME,   bottom on BOVARY flavor of the
ink nesting in his gums   tongue across every inch

of page   it was limp, wet
He jammed it in his mouth,   chewing,
rabid possum   on barely breathing flesh,
pulp on edge of tongue   smeared
on his   teeth,

hard palate,   then soft

Burn Baby, Burn

Amber wasn't allowed to play in the Issa Eight house. It was a forbidden white Queen Anne elephant, tall with thin, brittle bones. Its snout shot long in the air, a turret jutting out from a black roof line. The porch was covered in spindles, paint rubbed raw to gray like sharp broken teeth. She wasn't allowed to play there but if she stood, toes touching the base board of that first step to the porch, no one could say she was *really* being bad. And, if she turned her head a certain way, cocked it a little, just a little, so the wind caught her ear, she could just barely hear it. The percussion of a woman's heel on a clean hardwood floor. A man's braying laughter. No, she wasn't allowed to play inside the Eight House. But, really, it isn't playing, visiting your dead.

The town talked, chittering voices like squirrels safe up high on the branch, telling stories of the night the Issa House, that old ridiculous seat at 8 Birdsong Lane, burned itself out. The Issas had always held the castle. It sat up high on the hill, overlooking the town but like her Aunt Val said, no one likes to be looked down on.

Those same people always forgot, or thought not to mention, that more than the Issa's died that night. The town began to slough off layers of skin. Ash from the fire drifted down the hill and settled over the town. The mill closed down. Then, the little strip mall on the Boulevard went vacant. By the time the second-run movie theater had shuttered its doors, people had begun to sneer at what the castle had become.

Amber's older cousin, Kayla, would lie and say she remembered all the happenings inside the Eight House just because she was four years older than Amber. But, they were just babies when the fire spread through - Amber had just turned two the night before. They both

3

could have been burned up, turned to ash and dust like the walls on the inside. Somehow, Val got them out before the fire picked the staircase clean. No one else made it out of the Eight alive.

After the fire, Val took the insurance money, what little was left after the burials and doctor's visits and bought one of those modular houses. It had a foundation; it wasn't just some trailer. They were never trailer trash. How can you be when the sun still glints across the sooty windows of the Eight House? The little house was just a make-do place, set up in the long shadow of the Eight. But, that's what the Issas' did, they made do. And, they always held the castle.

"Darling," Val said to Amber, her hand cupped around a Virginia Slim as she lit the tip. "Darling, put that animal down. It doesn't want you." She stretched the words out, like syrup dripping through a sieve. The tabby cat wiggled and squirmed in Amber's arms and she held tight, tighter, until she could feel little rib bones moving and shifting inside the cat's body. She rubbed her leathery cheek against soft, dirty fur. "Darling, that's Kayla's cat. Leave her be."

Amber timed her breathing, inhaling as Val exhaled. She pulled that acrid pang of exhaust into her own lungs. She imagined it was Val's soul leaving her body, entering her own. She let the cat go, soft paws jumped over Amber's shoulder and landed, streaked across the lanai and through a hole in the bushes.

"You love too hard," Val said to her, shaking her head. "You hold too tight."

Val went back inside, letting the screen door slap closed. Amber heard her yell out to Kayla, telling her to turn her God damn music down. Amber left the lanai, left the looming shadow of the Eight and into the bright sunlight. She watched Val's chickens for a while as they ate ticks out of the yard. It looked like someone had thrown a handful of river rocks out in the grass, all white and tan and brown. She picked up a piece of gravel from the driveway, tossed it at the cluster of hens. They squawked away from her in a flurry of loose feathers.

4

Looking up at the Eight, it was almost possible to believe it was whole and safe. That it wasn't a shallow husk, a dead hollow seed left fallow in the field. That it was a home. Amber walked over and stood at that first step, watching bugs crawl up and over the rotting wood. She liked to watch the ants build and rebuild their homes after a barefooted giant had come in, demolished everything. Those ants start, grain by grain to rebuild. She couldn't see the trail of scent they left behind, etched into the dirt so others would know to follow, but she knew something was driving them to one another.

The smell of wet soot and ash swept out of the broken front door of the Eight and she thought about the ants, going home, rebuilding. She stepped up once, smashing the ants in place with her dirty bare feet. She stepped up again, wooden planks groaning. Somewhere inside, a trail of wet soot and ash had the power to take Amber to her family. She believed it.

"What are you doing?" Kayla asked from behind. She wore one of Val's old skimpy string bikinis, stars and stripes, and cat-eye sunglasses. In her arms, she carried a green beach towel, a bottle of baby oil and a tall icy glass bottle of Pepsi. The bathing suit bagged at the butt where the elastic had started to give out. Kayla's breasts were just beginning to sprout into little buds beneath the flagged stars of her top.

"Nothing," Amber said and dropped down off the stairs. She rubbed a hand against the pink cotton shirt at her belly and looked around to be sure Val wasn't behind Kayla anywhere.

"You know you aren't allowed in there," Kayla said and carried her towel over into the grass. Amber sat down on the bottom step and began to scoot her butt up and backwards, crab-walking up each step like a dare. *Not the boss of me*, she thought. Kayla laid her towel out in the sunlight, laid herself down. She began to slather the baby oil on her smooth tan legs. Amber cocked her head, tried to hear the ghosts of the Eight as they caught on the wind. Sometimes they liked when she sang to them so she crooned and stood to dance on the porch like one of Val's mangy brown chickens.

5

The rotting porch was a stage; the town below, a theatre in the round. And behind her, in the wings, she could feel her parents waiting, waiting for her to join them in the crossover.

"Burn Baby, Burn Baby," Amber sing-sang it under her breath, trying to coax the spirits out.

"What is wrong with you?" Kayla asked, bolting up straight, her back rigid. "Why are you singing that?"

Amber shrugged. She'd heard the other kids singing it in town and it had gotten stuck in her head, an endless loop of repeating verse. She smiled at the way the words fit in her mouth, like a piece of chewy fat on a pork chop bone. It was her favorite when they'd yell, "Burn Baby, Burn Baby, BURN!" Such a hopeful cheer at the end, like pom poms waving or parade candy being thrown out to the curb. Everything burns.

"You idiot," Kayla said. "They are singing about you."

Amber shrugged again and sang it louder. She could hear movement inside the Eight House and stamped hard on the wooden planks of the porch, bent her knees and stomped again. She twirled around and around like the little pink ballerina on the wind up jewelry box Val had given to her on her eighth birthday. With each passing loop, she began to see the blur of faces, such beautiful glowing faces, staring out from the huge bay window overlooking the porch of the Eight. The wind began to push against her, urging her on, telling her to go, go, spin.

"Stop it!" Kayla screamed and threw one of her flip flops at Amber. "God!" she flopped back down and covered her eyes with her oily arm. Amber stopped spinning and the wind died down, the faces of her dead withdrew back into the darkness of the house. Amber ran a finger over her own arm, puckered with scars, red and white, mottled bright like the stars on Kayla's swimsuit. The burn ran up her left arm, over her shoulder and neck, across her chin and cheek. The skin never stopped feeling tight, stretched thin and wrinkled.

6

"Burn Baby, Burn Baby," Amber whispered, looking right at the entrance of the Eight. Right at the singed Mahogany front door and busted out transom windows. Keep out signs were bolted to the door frame. The front porch was dropped low from a crack in the foundation, that drooping elephant face shifted forward and falling, teeth biting out into the dirt in desperation.

Kayla sighed. "Look, come over here, will you?"

Amber turned, jumped down off the porch and walked over to where Kayla lay in the yard. Amber dropped down beside her and Kayla eased away, back onto her elbows. Kayla had her hair up in a long brown pony tail, tied high like a thick mane. Val said Amber's hair was dirty dishwater blond. So thin, and thinning, like silver tinsel on a Christmas tree. Every morning Val would fight and scrape Amber's hair back with a rat tailed comb until Amber would cry out.

"Those kids," Kayla began but stopped. Amber sat and waited, watched as a bird carried mud up to the aluminum spouting on the Eight. "Those kids aren't being nice to you."

Amber caught her tongue in her teeth and picked at the long blades of grass. Kayla continued. "They hit you. Even like that, with words or whatever. They hit you but you don't got to stay hit."

Amber looked up. "What do you mean?" she asked Kayla but the words were already tumbling around in Amber's head. "Don't stay hit." It was a new song in her head.

"Well, it means, if someone hits you, you got to hit them back. Or they won't never stop hitting you." Kayla picked up her bottle of Pepsi and the cold sweat around the base of the bottle dropped on her chest. She wiped it away, oil and water, and took a deep drink. As she gulped it down, Amber could hear little tiny bubbles popping in Kayla's throat. Kayla took a breath to clear the bubbles before continuing, "And with your face, someone's always gonna want to be hitting it."

That night, after Val had chased Amber into bed, yelling for her to brush her teeth, Amber heard the front door of the Little House creak open and smack closed. The walls of the Little House were thin like

7

sheets of tissue paper. If she pressed a hand against her bedroom wall, she could imagine it tearing through to the other side. She crept from bed and peered out into the dark hallway, heard Val giggling behind the closed door of her bedroom. From within, the timbre of a man's voice registered. "Come back, baby," he said. "Come on back over here. I got something here for you."

"I already seen that," Val said but Amber heard the bed springs squeak as someone lowered down onto the bed.

Amber eased out into the hall and walked barefoot into the kitchen. She was so quiet, mouse-stepping to the refrigerator and pulled out the heavy jug of milk. She watched the hallway, listening for movement, as she gulped a glass of milk down. Val never let her have anything to drink after ten because of the accidents. Most of the time, Amber was able to hide her sheets but her bedroom had begun to smell like old pee. She had covered the wet with a towel but the mattress was yellowing to brown. The smell had begun to rot out into the hallway. So, she knew for sure, Val would slap her hand with the old green fly swatter if she caught her sneaking drinks.

Amber refilled her glass of milk and began again to drink. Her belly was full but she couldn't stop until the glass was empty. Maybe this time, if Val slapped her, she wouldn't have to stay hit. Maybe this time, Val would feel the grate of the fly swatter against her own skin. Amber smiled into her shadow, cast out by the light of the open refrigerator. She set her glass into the sink, full already with dirty dishes and crusted bits of food, and climbed her way onto the counter top. She reached up to the top of the refrigerator and fumbled around until she found the dingy fly swatter. She whooshed it around in the air, a streak of green and white.

She froze when she saw the fire. From the window above the sink, she could see the flames shooting out high and smoke billowing out in black curls as it belched from the upstairs windows of the Eight House. She crawled over dirty dishes and pressed her face against the cool glass of the window. Embers rained down like a brilliant red snow

8

storm, swirling and inviting. She ran to the back door and out onto the patio. The cement floor felt hot beneath her feet but when she looked up at the Eight, all she saw was darkness. The fly swatter still in hand, she stepped out into the night.

A barn owl called out, a deep hooting whoop before it screeched out a warning. It was a terrible sound, full throat and high pitched. The owl flew overhead and landed on the roof of the Eight. It's head swung all the way around, white feathers illuminated by silver moonlight.

Amber walked up to the porch, taking each step in slow, careful movements. From deep within the Eight, something began to call. "Burn Baby, Burn Baby," it sang out, a melody pulled from the ash. She wasn't allowed to play in the Issa Eight House, she knew that. But, as she stepped across the threshold and the fire lit up behind her, casting sparks of cinders out onto the porch like fireflies, she smiled. It isn't playing, is it? Needing the dead?

9

Game For Two

Games that you and I can play – how about
the Lion Tamer, you spread my jaws and fearlessly
thrust your head into my gaping mouth –

or the Hardboiled Egg, juggle me, blow on me,
smack me down hard and roll me back and forth
on a flat surface –

or the Strip of Textured Wallpaper, size me up,
shake me straight, press me firmly against the wall,
smooth out all my bumps and bubbles.

But you shake your head irritably and so it will
be the same game as last night and the night before,
the Extremely Cerebral American novel,

and you'll work your way through me, not really
enjoying me that much but relishing the feeling of
cognitive enrichment, secure in the knowledge

that you won't be embarrassed at the monthly
meeting of the Suburban Ladies' Book Club, whose
members can be so Booker Prize snobby.

And though we've played this game a hundred times,
I don't really mind indulging you again, because
eventually you'll fall asleep on your back,

light still on, me lying open on your breast, your steady breathing gently stirring my pages, my spine cracking pleasurably with every rise and fall.

Bones

Most women hate bones. They recoil biting fragments stuck in meat. "You're carving all wrong," my wife scolds. For women, bones flash the chain of life: birthing in fields; sucking on teats; playing till the sun sets; getting trucked to the slaughterhouse at the edge of town.

Men don't mind bones. If I hit a frag I spit it out like a bullet. Perhaps bones link us to our primal pasts, such as hunting mammoths with spears on icy plains. Back at the cave, women imagine death watching a girl drag a charred bone over the wall. They learn how to whisper.

Chicken Littled

So I'm on my bed playing, maybe action figures or Legos when my brother comes barreling in from behind me and I know it's him by the names of his arms those marks there—his tattoos and freckles and he won't let me turn around, I think this his game where younger brother gives creed to older—his strength, a tidal wave that comes up strong against the thin framed strength of me and I crumble—he's saying I can't hear what the television says—it's about prophecy, a strange new word to young ears, but it's too late for I've heard over and over again about the TV and its mouth talking Nostradamus's meteors, but my brother's hands come up anyway and close off my ears and against him and his brute force, I struggle, and the world outside is crying the future in ruination and my brother hums and hums to fill my head with a childhood of the always future.

On the Good Ship Explorer of the Seas

That would be on the picnic table
And the crowd bursts into wild applause - a match
For a moment all the silly moves the cruise director pushed
From bingo to the single's mingle to the art auction
Comes together with a sweet unity in the theatre
That would be on the picnic table the old man matches his wife's
      response
Most unusual place where the couple made 'whoopee'?
Whoopie that wonderful word that puts sex into the conversation with
      a smile
His wife of 66 years gives him a gentle kiss
And the crowd knows something special here
Not the canned side shows of the cruise
'World's sexiest man' - 'Belly flop contest' - 'Casino jackpot'
A friend calls it 'sweet' and I think too small
This about collective surprise…collective understanding
We so wish for that stadium moment - the home run and all that
Here it appears within the frame of a silly game
Greg Moglia On the Good Ship Explorer of the Seas
His wife reaches for his hand
And as they walk off stage
The crowd now standing
At full joy

Pending Harvest

The yellow-gold wave of the bean plants meant that shortly Jake Turner would return.

Thetis sat on her father's porch, an October wind fluttered the low-slung leaves, the sun thickening quickly. Puff clouds huddled in the fine, cerulean sky. An aching, musty scent of pumpkin drifted. Amber like sorghum spilled over the after-dinner hour, almost cold enough for a shawl. The shawl she'd made from snippets of worsted wool, close hand-work, spun carrot-colored. The shawl she'd worn for the Worleytown Social. She'd stood sentry at the punch bowl with Eliza Cane, the punch bowl that had a straight-shot to the door that any minute Jake Turner might walk through.

Jake Turner, it was said, had invested out West, like he had in the beans here. That's why he couldn't be here. Folks said, "Jake Turner's got a fine mind and so strapping, too! He's one blessed by the Almighty! Already he's doubled the seed money his Uncle Jones-Worthington leant him."

"Jake Turner," a whippet of a girl with dish brown hair and a bonnet declared as she gathered the punch cup between both gloved hands, "has a girl out there with straw-colored hair—very, very pretty and a blue ribbon huckleberry pie baker for all of Hascolm County. Cousin Mary Alice heard from Tucker Kimbrough that he's going to bring her back. Word is, they're soon to be promised. "

Thetis didn't like the way the whippet girl said that. The girl had a mean punch of glee in her voice as she announced it like Gospel truth. As Thetis stirred that oversize spoon through the punch bowl, she decided that the girl's face had a horsey-high forehead and a weasel's hunger to gnaw. A face like that could be counted on for nothing but gossip and lies.

Eliza Cane said, "It probly wasn't true, anyway," as she gently coaxed the spoon from her friend to take over spinning the sugar water. That was Eliza, true blue. Thetis kept glimpsing watch of the entrance, just in case. Three girls in a huddle from Miss Jackson's Sunday School. A parent. Mrs. Baxer-Barnes shaking droplets of rain from her overcoat and parasol.

From her father's porch, Thetis watched the crumbly bean stalks, like so much fake gold, glimmer. Looking out, even a smart one could be fooled. Hadn't Jake Turner, the very Sunday before he'd gone west, accompanied her home from the picnic on the pretext of checking on his tenant's mule?

"I find it best to keep on the top of things," he'd said, proud froth of brown hair and those eyes that hurt her like staring too hard at the sun—they left a pleasant, bright burn—and Thetis had nodded, as if she or any of hers knew about tenants and stock. Thankfully, she'd put on her sister's hand-me-downs and scrunched her feet up with each step to keep Gladys' shoes from flopping too hard. What would Jake Turner think if he knew sometimes she walked these backwoods to Miller's Pond barefoot?

Thetis knew this land, though her family didn't own it. Sometimes, she'd light out once chores were done—Baby Sister fed, creek water fetched, dish after dish ladled with vegetables or a hunk of hunted rabbit meat, dipped in flour and crisped. If you got still enough, various critters would draw near—sometimes a fawn with wobbly steps, other times a cottontail her brothers had missed, once a beaver with whittled funny teeth.

Jake Turner had a funny sense of getting ahead in life that he carried every moment, like a promise he'd deliver on. Unlike the boys who were just boys, Jake Turner was a boy who seemed like a man. But he wasn't that old, he'd once gone to fourth grade with her older

16

brother, Johnny, though Johnny'd had to drop out to start work at the mill.

On the Sunday before Jake Turner left, they'd proceeded along the path, her shoulders only just tipping his chest. In her chest, the spun gold feeling. Jake Turner talking now and then about beans and how to know when they were ripe and when it was past their time and such, but mostly, they walked in tandem in silence, like in all their walks. He'd almost grabbed her hand, almost touched her, handing back over the pail with the fresh eggs her mother had bid her to get and which he insisted to let him carry. Their hands had almost touched on the handle, lingering, of the pail.

"I find it best to walk a lady back, if that's all right by you." She'd looked down at the dirt path, that amber sunlight all through her, the delight that burned the everyday green into spun gold. She'd nodded.

Jake Turner might have gone, but that almost-touch had to mean something. His appearing along that path before going west, it had to mean something. The way he'd said, "I find it best to walk a lady back," it had to mean something.

"What that girl said probly wasn't true, anyway," Thetis assured herself, on her father's porch, overlooking the field of sharecropped beans her father tended, it meant something. Even if Jake Turner hadn't returned for the social. By harvest, Jake Turner would return to check on his investment. It wasn't true, what the horse-face girl had said. She was mean-spirited and a lying gossip. He would remember their walks, he would remember the last walk before he'd gone West, when their hands had almost touched.

Jake Turner would return alone. Alone, she repeated to the wind, to no one. He would. It had to mean something— the beans, the walks, that yellow-gold feeling.

17

The Sticky Grid

The little girl felt her mother's sorrow
ooze into the kitchen like batter
along the rim of the waffle iron,
palest ochre blackened at the burnt edges
against the silver metal. The girl knew
that her mother's pin-curled head
often filled with memories
of her own mother glaring at her
with apple seed eyes, telling her,
"You're selfish, rotten."

But how could sorrow exist with the warm syrup
welling in the waffle's tiny squares
set out on knockoff Delft? Wasn't sorrow
like gnats swirling in humid air that bit you
and flew up your nose?
How could sorrow be there with morning
fresh-squeezed orange juice, its glistening
pulp, only a pit or two bobbing in the glass?

Wasn't sorrow supposed to stalk in at night
like a hissing cat, back arched?
Or was that anger with its pointed teeth,
spiny tongue, and drilling blue eyes?

The girl told her mother three knock-knock jokes,
but her mother didn't smile. While the girl licked

the syrup welling in the waffle's square pools,
she thought of the sparrow that once flew
into the open window, darting to each ceiling corner.
When she tried to coax it out, it throbbed
as it flew, bashing itself against the pane
again and again.

Library Girl

In college, I obsessed about free will. I wondered, if you knew at the beginning where you end up, would you live a different life? If you could see over the horizon, would you change, is what I wondered. But now, I think that we live the lives we need to live even if we end up in a ditch.

Still, it's funny how things turn out. My first semester at college, a small school in Florida, I had a mad crush on a boy named Byron Porter. My crush began at a moonlit party by the swimming pool when parties were new to me, with their noise and music and everyone jumping up and down. Everybody drank scotch and smoked pot and swam around. In Florida, when the evening is warm, it's thrilling to gaze at a starry sky.

Late at night, Byron Porter swam next to me, like a fish, and we kissed. I wished we could go on kissing under the stars forever, that's how it felt.

For the next few months, I'd close my eyes at night and imagine the kiss, even after there were far graver things on my mind. Byron Porter, with his black hair in ringlets falling to his shoulders, reminded me of a picture of The Three Musketeers I had seen once, maybe in a Classics Illustrated comic. Byron was stoned most of the time and had no reason to recall one party more than another. He never led me to think that he remembered the swim.

Byron Porter had a best friend—Leo Hubbard, another tall string-bean hippie. It was wonderful to see them, together, playing their guitars, laughing, stoned. Both were brainy in math, although, as everyone knew, Byron was the genius, the one all of the girls chased.

Besides, he had that magical Southern accent that made everything sound like a poem.

From the sidelines, I watched their parade of girlfriends. Byron's girls became pale from staying indoors all the time, hidden in his refrigerated room. They emerged in the evenings, stoned, mostly on acid, looking like creatures from the moon. Leo's romantic interests were a weird bunch—one left school insanely chatting to spirits about a lettuce-only diet, another changed her sex, and yet another turned into a high-priced call girl in LA. Leo seemed drawn to loonies—like many kind normal people, he craved a bit of insanity.

Leo Hubbard and I had become friends as he courted my friend, Louise Moon. Leo would position himself beneath her window with his guitar, crooning a ditty which was along the lines of Please, Louise, Jeez, Louise, something like that. He was a sight. Beautiful Louise was fond of Leo, but soon, her spirit world intervened and she was sent away. Leo was morose after she left, and he and I spent many an hour chatting about fate, free will and other matters.

About a year after that moonlit kiss, Byron Porter and I were in-between romances. I had seen little of him, since, as I mentioned, he'd been locked away in his frozen quarters with one pale girl after another. In daylight, he looked like a ghost student. The rest of us were tanned and fit.

One day, Byron said to me, his voice all rumbling and throaty, "I'm thinking about you all the time."

By that time, I knew something about myself and I knew I was not by nature a party girl. I was more of a library girl, if you know what I mean. "There are more interesting things to think about in this world. I am studying the mind-body problem this term."

"That's what I'm thinking about, how you say things like that," he murmured. His pitch-dark eyes were something.

"Byron, you are sexy, that's the truth."

21

"That's not a bad thing." Byron laughed in his sad way. His father had shot himself and his sister had gone crazy, so he had what to laugh about.

"It's neither good nor bad. It's an empirical fact." I was, after all, a philosophy major.

"I think you're sexy, and that's definitely not a bad thing," was his answer as he moved closer. We were standing in front of his room.

"It's not bad, but it's not important. You place too much importance on physical experience, you need to think about the Mind."

"There's nothing wrong with your mind," Byron said.

Up close, he smelled like tobacco and pot all mixed up. But, I had no desire to repeat the kiss—it could only be an inferior version of the first perfect kiss, or so I feared. Another kiss, in harsh daylight, could only disappoint.

"Listen, some man's going to break my heart, but it won't be you, it will be someone else. Anyway, you shouldn't stay indoors so much, it's not good for you," I said.

He murmured my name—the way he stared back at me, I almost wavered. He stood absolutely still, waiting until I edged away and put space between us. He wouldn't press the point, I knew. And then he slipped into his dark room. Soon after, I saw him around with another pale girlfriend.

* * *

Many of us floundered after graduating, but not Byron. He was snatched up for a plum job in New York banks—Citi or Chase, I cannot recall. The work was hardly enough to keep someone like Byron busy, even if he was high half the time. He had time to kill, as he put it. And that turned to be enough time for him to create a program that automated his work, along with the work of dozens of others, which he craftily sold back to his employer. With the cash, he formed a company, Holistics.

It was a given that Leo would join him, as an almost equal partner, not fifty-fifty, but close. Leo was in L.A. waiting in vain for his call-girl

22

lover to quit her crazy life and marry him. Leo flew back, with some regret—he worried about the girl, alone in L.A.

They up ended working in London for a few years. At first, Leo was homesick. His idea of foreign was Mexico: spicy food, sunny beaches, gaudy colors. But in his letters, he wrote that he and Byron had gotten used to warm beer, chilly weather and English women. They had fallen in love.

Back in New York, Leo invited me to his wedding. "There's nothing special about her, except I love her," he said of his wife-to-be.

"She must be special if you love her, and I know she's lucky. And how is Byron?"

"That's a mess. He married some woman who stole funds from the bank," he said. "And I couldn't talk any sense into him, no way, you know Byron."

I gathered that the marriage had helped the wife avoid jail. "I guess she's beautiful," I said, figuring something must explain this unlucky choice. Byron was always stoned, but never shady.

"Pretty enough, but not as pretty as you, if that's what you're asking. And are you still with what's his name."

"It depends on what you mean by with," I replied. "And that wasn't what I was asking."

Leo finished his beer. "Women," he said, dazed.

Leo had a large country-style wedding in upstate New York, about five hours out of the city. His mother and aunts had cooked up a storm, and long picnic-style tables were laid out with ribs and chicken and cherry pies. Leo and Byron played guitar together, looking as joyful as men can. Byron's pretty wife was far too pregnant to dance, so he hugged her as if they were dancing. All in all, it seemed like a storybook ending or where you expect the story to end.

* * *

Byron's decision to quit came out of the blue. For the first time, the two men argued, and as with all fights about money, it was drawn-out and bitter. Leo had drawn only a modest salary, reinvesting every

23

penny—and Byron demanded cash on the spot, for his share. The years of friendship, years of hanging out and playing music—to Byron, these were nothing, or at least not enough to soften him.

Or, so I heard from Leo. I was not a lawyer or anything like a lawyer, but I had a logical way of thinking that he could count on. Besides, Leo trusted me to consider his interests alone.

I'd imagined that Holistics was Byron's show, but Leo told a different story. "His algorithms got us started, but he hasn't done any real work since then. He shows up to meetings only when he wants to, I never know what he's doing," Leo said, as if speaking of a delinquent child.

"I guess the only question is, can you keep the clients without him?" I asked.

"I basically run the company for all intents and purposes. As far the clients are concerned, Byron's some weirdo in the background."

"Byron's not going change his mind. Find people to buy him out. If you don't, you'll end up paying him for the rest of your life. You need a clean break," I said.

"I can find investors, no problem. But Byron owns most of the company, so whoever buys his share has control, and there's not much cash around. And if we go that route, I don't want to speak to Byron again. I don't want anything to do with him," Leo said. He had a mild temperament, even his anger was muted.

"That's the only way. Byron's not your problem," I argued and I believed what I said.

And that was that for a while. The company prospered and eventually went public—and fortunately, the new owners kept Leo on board as CEO. From what I gathered, Byron left New York and severed contact with everyone. For years, I heard nothing of Byron Porter.

* * *

More than a decade passed before I next met Leo Hubbard—after many false starts, we'd managed to arrange lunch. But first, I dropped by to see his glossy office in midtown Manhattan, so ultra-modern and bare, it might have been a spaceship. The one remnant of the old office was a poster of Florida, the type with hot-pink flamingos and an orange sunset.

Leo looked much the same, if beardless and not as skinny. But his eyesight, even in college, had never been strong. Now, he mentioned a variety of vision problems, as if speaking of another frailer man in a distant hospital.

We were getting ready to leave when a young woman rushed in, dressed in the way that college girls dress in a too-flimsy top with black leggings. She and Leo had some whispered exchange in computer-speak: some fragment of code had gone missing or was broken or corrupted. I played with my Blackberry as they spoke, to give them privacy.

But then, she turned around. I saw the long dark ringlets and pitch-dark eyes that were happy and sad at the same time, and I knew who she must be. Of course, Leo and Byron had been in touch—I should have known.

"Jewel Porter, she's heard about you," Leo said. "She's going to Columbia in the fall, math genius like Byron."

"You look like your father. I hope he's doing well."

"If you call living in a trailer OK, he's OK," she said, looking at no one. Her voice, low and rumbling like Byron's, evoked smoky rooms, melancholy ballads.

I was trying to put the word trailer together with Byron and I heard Leo explaining, "Byron's living in his family's backyard in a trailer, and Jewel's mother is back in England. She's remarried to an old friend of ours, well, he used to be my friend." He mentioned a familiar name— no one special, not like Byron, an average-looking guy they'd hired in London.

"And the money?" I asked. Money was only part of the story, but Byron had been paid enough to last most men a few lifetimes and then some.

25

"I guess that's in England too," Leo answered slowly. "No one knows for sure, not Byron, anyway. No one's traced it, not that anyone's tried."

I could fill in the blanks, bits and pieces of a life flying apart, landing who knows where, in somebody's backyard—and all the time, this radiant daughter, watching.

"Leo, I went to a psychic in the Village the other day," Jewel said. "I found her online. She's famous. She knew all about what happened to Byron, where he'd been, where he was. She told me, watch out, be careful." She lifted herself to the window's ledge, so that she could be higher than us. Behind her was a ceiling-high window that faced the skyline.

"That could mean anything," I said. Jewel gave a tiny merciless nod from her perch, as if to say, *obviously.*

"Or nothing," said Leo. "You can't predict. Like you drop a ball, and you think it's going to hit the floor. You think: it's gravity, it falls. But someone grabs it and it never hits the ground. That's like me. I was falling apart when Byron asked me to join the company. And it was a million to one, maybe a billion to one even, that I'd be here with all of this."

"But you couldn't save him," said Jewel and her eyes glazed over the ordinariness of me, in my black fashionable suit.

I felt attacked, even though she had directed her comment at Leo. "Byron was the one who was in charge. No one thought he needed saving."

"No one thought or no one bothered to think?" Jewel asked. "You have no idea, do you? You have no concept of who he is, who he actually is."

Funny thing was, a concept of Byron was all that I had. There was Byron in his ghostly space, music blaring, shades drawn to block sunlight, in one darkened room after another—was one room all that different, really? To Jewel, the differences were vast, frightening, but to Byron?

26

"Maybe," I said. "But you're here now. I'm guessing that Byron sent you to Leo, right?"

"Of course," she answered casually. "It was a given that I'd come here, after I got the scholarship to Columbia. Leo's done everything."

I couldn't help but blow a kiss to Leo, and mouth, thank you, thank you, thank you. There weren't enough thank yous in me.

Jewel looked at me as if I had just entered the room. "I guess you were in love with my father. Everyone was, weren't they?"

"Not me, I was more of a library girl," I told her.

"Was it the drugs?" she asked.

It was natural that she had a romance about her father, a grand decadent sort of romance. Perhaps in her secret fantasies, the ones only she knew about, she met a man like him and destroyed herself as she imagined he had, slowly, cruelly, deliberately. Well, I wouldn't touch that.

"No, it wasn't drugs—it was kind of a mind body problem," I said and drifted off to swimming pools and starry skies. I was facing the poster with the sunset: corals, turquoises, yellows, corny as a Hallmark card. But that's how Florida looks, it can't help itself. "Leo, it's strange that you kept this. It spoils the whole urban industrial vibe."

"You don't remember?" Leo asked with the smile that he kept in reserve for me.

I had a memory of him and Byron with newly short hair, wearing lumpy parkas, a threatening grey sky as they disappeared into a dark subway entrance. I hadn't asked where they were going.

"You gave it to me. I hated the city when I got here, it was so dirty and cold and I thought I'd go crazy, cooped up in an office. So you brought me this poster and we hung it up together, me and Byron and you. And you said: Imagine you're in an office and there's one window, and outside, it's Florida, outside, there's a sunset, outside there's the bay and there's flamingos and pink clouds, it's a perfect day. And as long as you're inside, you won't feel so lonely." Leo almost laughed and said, "You still get that faraway look."

27

"I was an impossible girl," was all I could say.

"Impossible," Jewel repeated. And she turned to catch a glimpse of the new moon— faintly visible for a moment, but too far away to matter.

That Guy

Peter always waits for them to come to him. And, one by one, they always do. He waves to the barman to hit him again. A brunette who was always given her birthday present a full week late, cuts through her conversation to catch his eye. One by one, they come to him. Peter dog-ears the brunette. There is a different kind of special someone he has been waiting for. Ah, look. There's that someone now. Johnny enters through the red velvet curtain, looking like he has been drafted. It's time for Johnny to get out a little. Seriously. It's time. Peter is that guy who the wives never want their husbands hanging around. But, Peter has been waiting. He just knew that, one by one, they would all eventually come back to him.

Into the Mirror

As an artist I play with myself,

imagining thick oil paint

smeared between my breasts.

I look in the mirror,

my fat—strokes of burnt umber and raw sienna.

I highlight my imperfections with the tip of my finger.

Each stroke outlines my frame resting on the sheets,

but as a woman I hold my body close

just hoping he likes what he sees.

Actor Singer Model Voice

These were the descriptions you listed below your name on your casting card. The one you pulled out of your purse and slid across the table to me, after I'd asked you what kind of theater you'd done. This question of mine was precipitated by your admission--let's face it, confession—about acting on the side to your office job in Marketing, the main capacity in which I know you.

I don't know why you did it. Flashed me this incongruously intimate slip. I think I saw you think better of it midway through the reflexive gesture—which would have made sense if I was an agent or a theater director. But I wasn't. I was Brad from Sales. And this was a benefits update meeting.

The card had your face on it. Looking done up and dashing as a prom queen. The reddish hue on the matte finish and your swirling hair made you look like a cream colored rose with eyes. I looked at the back and saw your full, very married, name—Melanie Shubert Hantz. And all the things you were.

Actor Model Singer Voice.

The attributes were all lined up together on the card. Like pop dream identities God let you pick out from the aisles of his toyland in a kind of pre-life haze.

Reading them made me wish I had a similar card reading:

Drop-out, Bar hopper, Hubby, Rep.

My autobiography in five words. My wife said she'd read an anthology of those once, but could only remember one by Hemmingway about baby shoes for sale, never used.

Your card also had your phone number on it. You saw me notice.

I flipped the card over to look at your picture again.

31

I heard you squirm a little. Shift in your wool pants. Snicker self consciously. You were laughing at yourself for bothering to show me. Maybe you were laughing at me for being voyeur enough to look again right in front of you.

Now what? I thought to myself. Slide the card back and make you feel like a ditz?

I didn't feel like watching you bashfully stashing it back into your clutch. But I also didn't feel like creeping you out by pocketing it. *What's his wife going to think if she finds that?* I didn't want to give you the satisfaction of thinking yourself a home wrecker. You're way too sweet. Way too ordinary. I wasn't going to let you get tickled pink. You didn't deserve it.

So I let it sit in the middle of the table, refusing to look at you for the next half hour as we heard about our portfolios and diversified retirement plans.

Meanwhile, I hatched a perfect lie to save us both.

"Say," I began. "Do you mind if I show your card to a friend whose thinking of re-doing his? His are glossy. And so. Well. L.A."

You were happy to oblige. "But they're really nothing special. Just the Free 200 business card thing online. But once I got to designing them, I hated their free templates, so I paid the ten dollars to get the better one."

"They got you with the buy up, huh?"

"Yeah, good sales right?"

I remembered you coming out to the showroom once about a month ago. On some assignment. You were impressed by my field work. And honest about your lack of people experience. Which I admired. You asked me some flattering, but starry eyed questions about outcomes and about buyers. All the wrong questions in my opinion. And, like a cat distracted with a ball of yarn, you started checking your phone the minute I began talking about what we actually sell.

You had a weird forehead. But I liked how thin you were and your ballet dancer's posture. Which I know now is from your acting classes.

32

You looked like someone existing to be seen by other people watching—me in this case. You looked back at me full on with your eyes as if waiting for me to define you. Your eyes were brown. Like my wife's.

Actor Model Singer Voice.

My wife is none of these. Her card reads:

Tom Boy, Laureate, Barista, Bride.

If you're living for people all the time, who are you when you're by yourself? My wife's the answer to this. She's herself and no other. Regardless of who's watching. She's body, being, soul. And because of this, she doesn't like more watchers than she can help and makes herself as plain as she can to ensure this. It's limiting for sure and we've had more than half of our fights about it. But I was the only one to ever break through that, motivated by mystery I guess. Only I will ever know her fully. This keeps me slightly separate from everyone I meet. Including you, whoever you are.

The meeting broke up. I tossed your calling card in my bag so I could shred it when I got back to the office. But I went out for a beer by myself after the meeting and didn't make it back to the office (and shredder) that day.

I set your card out on the countertop and looked at the names of things you said you were. Things of course, you weren't really. Things you were for a moment many years ago maybe. Things too numerous and ideal to ever pan out in this world at once.

I told myself not to look at your picture again.

I downed my beer.

I flipped over the card and looked at your picture again.

I found myself talking to you. That's where we are now, I'm afraid.

"So what else do you do?" your voice asks.

"Exist," I reply. Kind of Bogarty I know. But impossible to argue with.

"Come on. Tell me. Are you a writer? You seem like a writer," your voice asks.

33

"I'm nothing."

I think about leaving you there at the bar.

But I don't want some stranger picking you up. Especially if that stranger was you. If by chance you were to find yourself staring back at you, it'd make you feel bad. It would also reveal my lie without my motivations of saving us from something bad.

You might envision me at the bottom of a glass of beer having just had a conversation with your picture. Which would flatter no one. Flattery is our main duty to acquaintances. We leave things like contempt and vulnerability only to those who are intimate and committed to hurting and loving each other.

So I put you back into the bottom of my bag.

I put you there at the bottom of my bag so I can see your distant eyes occasionally. Staring up at me from the bottom of the place I go to look for things. So that in that moment, one that occurs every other day or so, I can say 'no' to knowing you. And in doing so, tell you who I really am.

Husband.

That's the only thing on my card. For now.

The Women of This Hot Rome

lift their hair off their necks
in double surrender: arms raised,
neck bared.

They can't maintain position
against me. Can't press back,
certainly not in this Santa Maria Maggiore
public square, as they celebrate Mary's Assumption
and her once giving badly needed snow in August.
What miracle today?

I have been in Florence
with the throng marching
up to the duomo, mindlessly
happy, prisoners of peace,
trading away the rapture
of belief for beauty.

Now, I maneuvered myself to the fourth
row as the women move from me
as if navigating a ski slalom post.

I am forty hungry days away from a woman,
and this pressing for better sight
pleases in another sort of double victory:
better views for the staff than the distaff.

35

In the square, monsignors and media specialists
will shoot fake snow out of a fake cannon;
I will see the whole explosion.

I rethink going to the museums
and churches instead of the clubs.

Why didn't I use the numbers my player
friends have given me?

The nuns are the most stolid obstacles
in their starched white and blue; nevertheless,
I press into row three, hear the pope
talk of the miracle, and am shocked
to feel a brief second-grade thrill.

This next blue habit will not give way.

There Are Angels

There are angels who might come
or might not
    Rains shine and keep
    the body turning
Winds dark
between the bed, the street,
    birdless sky

I'm a soldier at war with secrets and happiness
I've been up and down all night

We're a couple quite unlike ourselves
We drove back to Desert Moon Motel together

There are angels who speak
and some dumb
    Light has tedious work
    ahead today
Shadows leave
us to continental
    breakfast drinkies

I'm tipsy Jesus and should stop right here
I save waitresses with Irish coffee and cigarettes

We're a couple of runny eggs, over easy
We surround ourselves with bacon fat and hash

There are angels idling in pickups
in parking lots
    as the Mexican maid
    makes cheap beds
with chaffed hands
and marriages make
    their excuses

I'm at war, so unlike the desert tortoise
I've turned them on their backs in tender sun

We're already crowded with ruined light
We won't coax sleeping birds from our throats

There are numb-skulled angels pulling
their hell-bent squeaky trucks out and onto

    forgotten highways
There are angels who might come
                or might not

What If We Are All Monsters

I am normal and tall and I haven't brought my clothes to dress-out for gym since two weeks ago. I like gym, but I don't like to change in front of the other kids. When I was ten Father made Sister and I change in front of him before bed each night. I would help my sister's pants and shirt off, and then she would take off mine. I remember her skin would smell sweet. It was a welcomed scent compared to Father's sour breath. He would call me a 'sissy' and laugh at me when I was naked.

Its fucking Monday and Mrs. Humphries called on me five times today in class. She knows that I don't do my homework, so she calls on me to try to make me feel bad. I got three out of the five of her annoying questions right. I didn't feel bad at all.

Mrs. Humphries is married to Mr. Humphries; our gym teacher. Two weeks ago I walked into the back gymnasium to smoke a cigarette after second-block classes. Class bugs me silly and sneaking away to smoke in between helps me relax. There's a door that props open in the back of the gym and I can push all my exhales out of the crack. I always pretend that I am James Dean. I lift a cigarette up to my mouth; pinched between my forefinger and thumb. Then I slip my hand back down into my pocket and grab my box of matches. Striking one and looking around to notice all the people who aren't there to notice me.

I think like Dean would; *I'll bet I'm the most cold-blooded son of a bitch you could ever meet.*

Anyway sometimes when I'm smoking I'll hear things I'm not supposed to or sometimes see them. And this day, two weeks ago, while I was smoking, I heard a noise in the storage closet back by the rolled-up wrestling mats. I finished my cigarette and flicked it outside into the grass. Closing the door gently behind me, I walked over to the storage closet and turned the metal handle. The door was unlocked so of course I swung it open.

Mrs. Humphries' husband, Mr. Humphries, our gym teacher, is cheating on her with the school Softball coach. And man does Softball coach look good once she's shed.

So that's why I don't dress out for gym anymore.

* * *

Being a sophomore at high school is easy. It's easier than being a freshman, and easier than being a junior. It's just cooler in this year because in the first one you have to prove yourself and in the last two you gotta worry about what's next. You can fool anyone into thinking you are smart, and that gets you by. And it's all a number game; the teachers don't *really* care. They just want to get hired on again next year.

They have to keep their 'nine-to-fivers' so that their husbands keep giving them their two-story houses and golden retrievers. And at night when they sit at the dinner table over take-out pizza and talk about how their day went, Husband knows that Wife was working at school all day. And Husband gets off his six-figure-job at six, and Wife at five, so Husband knows Wife isn't cheating on him. And if Wife is, it's only for a really quick hour so it must not be all that good.

But they don't talk about this.

They chew their pizza crust and slurp down their twenty-five-dollar-bottle-of-wine that Husband brought home to surprise Wife.

Surprise...

Sometimes there is a girl I meet up with at school. Not my girlfriend though.

Her name is Cory and she draws on my arms with red and blue pens sometimes. She has a boy name and she sometimes she holds my hand when we walk around. One time we both got passes to get out of class. She was in second-block English and I was in Mrs. Humphries' math. Sometimes I would laugh thinking about how stupid Mrs. Humphries is—and she is supposed to be our teacher. But anyway, we both got passes at 11:14. She [the girl with the boy name] left me a note

40

in my locker and it said to meet her in the back gymnasium at 11:16. So I got my pass signed and went to meet her.

You have to walk past the boys and girls locker rooms on the way to the back gymnasium. So when I walk by I'll open the swinging doors and say, "Hello! Janitor, anybody in here?" Sometimes the girls are getting dressed and I can catch a glimpse of them before the scurry off. I just laugh and they scream and I just keep the pictures of them in my head.

When I got to the back gymnasium I gave Cory a cigarette, but she didn't want it. So I smoked mine, and then I smoked half of the one I pulled out for her. When I was done being Mr. Jammin'-James-Dean, she grabbed my arm and she took me into the storage closet. She told me that she liked me, and she put her hands down into my pants. I was wearing jeans and her bony wrists pressed into my stomach.

One time, at home, when Father made Sister take off my pants, she couldn't get the button undone and her knuckles pushed into my stomach as she struggled. I pushed [the girl with the boy name] off of me in the storage closet.

I liked Cory. As a friend. And I don't really know why I did that. But I did it, so whatever.

She left the storage closet whipping tears off her face and said she would never talk to me again. I sat on the floor for a minute and then got up and played janitor on my way back to class.

Not only do I not dress for gym, but if I don't want to, I don't even go anymore. Mr. Humphries is scared to look at me and when he does it's with a big-stupid-fat-white-guy-smile. He knows what I saw, and he doesn't know if I told anyone. Maybe if he pretends it didn't happen long enough he thinks I will too. It is funny he is so stupid—and he is supposed to be our teacher.

Instead of gym I will go to the tennis courts. I'll sit by myself and pull at the grass that pops up through the cracks. I twist it around my fingers and try to tie it into knots below my knuckles. It's fun to pull it tight until my skin turns white. Eventually the grass breaks though, and

41

I have to try another piece. Sometimes I bring chalk from the storage closet and I sit and draw on the court. Sometimes I will draw on my pants or on my hands too.

I know this girl named Maggie from school, and she plays tennis. She probably doesn't know me. Not by name anyway. One time I did the janitor trick on her and her friends and she saw me. I don't think her friends saw me but one of those stupid bitches told on me and Principle Yadayadayada had to talk at me forever.

Maggie is perfect.

She is a junior and she has big eyes and long legs and her boobs are bigger than all of her friends but she doesn't act like she knows that. She wears short jean shorts and the women teachers make her put her hands down to her side to test if they are too short. She always shrugs her shoulders up so that they look like they are long enough. She smiles her white teeth and tells them she has short arms. I've never seen a male teachers make her do that arm-test.

Sometimes when I'm on the tennis courts I draw pictures in chalk of Me and Maggie. Her stick-figures always have really long legs. I'll draw the pictures then I'll color on my pants. When I am wearing darker pants the chalk shows up really well. I'll start down my legs and draw lines up to my crotch. I'm in the drawing too sometimes.

I make sure to wipe it all off before I go back inside though.

So people don't think I'm a *weirdo*.

'Cus I ain't no weirdo!

* * *

I don't do anything after school, so once the final bell rings, I just walk back home. I like to walk by myself and I take the longest way possible. I walk past the pickup line where all the kids are getting into their parents big cars. And then I walk through the parking lot beside the license plates that say, '2QT-4U,' and 'CHSFB48' or 'UR-MOM' or 'TRSTNGOD' or 'MRMAN12'. From there I'll walk up the hill by the baseball field.

42

Behind the baseball field there's a pathway that leads through the woods to my neighborhood; Woodlawn Estates—How-Fucking-Fancy.

It's the same path that the other kids use to get to the football games so that they don't have to drive when they've been drinking. There's always beer cans and glass liquor bottles scattered along the trail. Sometimes I'll pick up the glass ones and throw them at the trees. They'll shatter and explode and the glass will shine in the sunlight.

There's a dog that used to be chained up on the trail. The owners that lived beside the pathway said that they measured the leash so that the dog was too far away to get to anybody. The dog was a German shepherd and it always barked and showed its teeth whenever anyone walked by. The groups that went by to football games didn't care because there were always so many of them it was like a game and they would laugh and run by. I always walked by myself.

But I didn't care either.

Sometimes I would go right up to the edge of the trail and call the dog. I would hold out pepperoni or potato chips in my hands and the dog would go crazy. He would jump up on his hind legs and yip and yap and snap and chomp at the air, but he was always too far. Every time I walked by I think the dog knew it was me and he always yanked on his chain and flashed his teeth. If I didn't have any food, I would just taunt him anyway as I walked by.

There's no more dog on the trail. Because one time he pulled so hard, his chain finally broke. I just happened to be nearby when it did. I might have had pepperoni in my hand or in my pocket.

I can't remember.

I was just walking by, minding my own business, like I always did. Not bothering the dog and he was like, barking like crazy at me.

For no reason.

Well I wasn't scared of the dog, and when his chain finally broke, he came after me. So I took out my knife that was in my pocket really fast and I made the blade go into the dog's neck. I didn't think it would

43

make his life stop, but he whined loud and fell to the ground and his barking stopped and his sincere blood was on my hand.

The owner's kid must have heard because he came outside and started to yell at me and curse at me. My shirt was red and there was hot red splatter on my hand and up my arm. I don't know why he was yelling at me and crying at me. I didn't do anything. All I do is walk by on my way back from school; minding my own business all the time.

"Oh what this? This Pepperoni and this beef-jerky? These are mine, they're my after school snack and I'm hungry so I had them out and I was eating them okay? Makes sense, man!"

The kid called me a liar and was really yelling at me, but I was bigger than him. Maybe not bigger but taller and I could see that he recognized it. I left my knife where it was in the dog's neck and I kept walking home. I chewed on the beef jerky and sometimes when the brown juices from the meat swelled up in my mouth I would spit them like the baseball players on TV do. I chewed and spit and walked the rest of the way home. I was upset that I had lost my favorite knife.

When I get home from school Father is never there and either is silly-Sister. My Father won't get home until it has been dark out for a while, and Sister normally stays after school for sports or clubs and stuff. She is blonde and tall and the boys think she is pretty. She fools people better than me.

I like to have the house to myself for a while. I can relax, and smoke, and go through Father's room to find his magazines. I probably first found them when I was eleven and I liked to look at them. I really liked to look at this one girl in them that reminded me of Maggie. Her name in the magazine was Penny Pretty and I thought that was such a beautiful name. She looked like how the girls looked when I walked into the locker room, except they were smaller and she was smiling. I ripped her picture out and stuck it under my pillow hoping that maybe I could dream about her.

I remember that night 'cus Father came in my room really late. He made my room smell like rubbing alcohol like instantly and he asked me if I had been looking at his magazines.

I told him no.

Penny Pretty was tucked in nicely underneath my pillow when Father came around by my bed. He had a glass bottle in his hand and he took a sip from it and then threw it against the wall in my room. It shattered and exploded.

"You like going through your Dad's stuff huh? You like fucking with his stuff when he's not home?"

He pulled the sheets off of me and yanked me up by my shoulders.

"Well let's just see how much you like going through Dad's stuff huh? Let's see if it's worth these thumpings" he said and I heard his belt clanking and unbuckling.

I don't remember what happened after that so I really can't talk about it. But I was sore when I woke up. When my Father saw me he just acted like he always did. Like nothing happened. Nothing really happened I guess.

But I still looked at Father's magazines. I just made sure that when I did I didn't crinkle the pages or tear any of them. And I made really careful that I didn't spill any of his lotion on them or when I finished with them I made sure that they weren't sticky or smudged. He would be upset again if he knew I was looking at them.

It was just nice to have some time to myself. And after looking at the magazines I would watch some TV or sometimes I would try to write in a journal or something. Doctor Carl says that writing is supposed to be helpful, but I don't know if he is really that smart. Father has money from when Mom died so he sends me and splendid-Sister to Carl to talk. I don't like to talk and Sister just says what she thinks she is supposed to.

If I get home from school by four-o'clock I can normally be done with the magazines by four-forty-five and then *Erratic* comes on MTV at five-o'clock. I don't try to be scheduled, but with school and

45

everything it works out that way sometimes. *Erratic* is a reality show where they put random people in situations where they freak out, like emotionally. I think its fake but I also think it is much more fun to watch knowing that. It's fun to see the actors pretend to have these spontaneous, erratic, terrified, silly, scared, surprised, deranged, angry emotions.

If it was actually genuine it might be terrifying.

But I keep it on in the background and listen to the narrator talk out in-between the screams or yells from blonde girls bouncing up and down. I'll turn through one of Father's magazines while I sit in his recliner and sometimes I fall in love again with the smiling girls stuck to the pages and I sneak away to my room to play again before Sister gets home. She normally gets home at six, but I turn the TV off anyway so I can hear her in case she comes home early.

When I am done with my after-school-extra-curricular-activities, I put on my Mr-Gacy-clown-suit and wash my hands. I have to be at work by seven but it is only a ten minute bike ride. I work under the nipple-less golden boobs in the drive-thru window, and I spit in people's drinks. I don't spit in everyone's, and not like, on purpose. If I have to sneeze or cough or anything I just don't make any effort to move their cups out from underneath my face. I don't like dressing up in an outfit based off of a clown with red hair, but it is nice because I can eat my dinner there and it gets me out of the house. I don't care much for the money but it helps because I don't have to ask Father for anything. I can buy my own cigarettes or whatever else I need.

The bike ride to the bronze-boobz is really my favorite part. I ride out of from my neighborhood Fancy-Fuckin'-Estates onto the main road and I get to go over the highway on the 'Lieutenant Martin 'Boomer' Bronstein Overpass'. Lieutenant Martin 'Boomer' Bronstein was some cop from town who got shot in the line-of-duty when I was a little kid. It was like a really big deal because it was some crazy kid who shot him. I remember the President got interviewed for our local paper and he mentioned where I live on TV.

46

So they gave the guy an overpass.

And people spray-paint stuff on it like dicks and gang signs and tags and 'wuz herez' that are more annoying than artistic. I just like going over the highway and feeling the wind gusts from the eighteen-wheelers. I'll get off my bike and walk it across and pretend that I am actually in the traffic below. The trucks come whizzing by at full speed right at my tall normal body but I always dodge out of the way in time and I only feel the wind spray as they speed past.

One time there was a boy from the Fox Burroughs neighborhood by the highway who didn't dodge in time though. I was crossing on my way to work one night and there were kids rolling empty cans out under the trucks passing by. I was walking my bike and I saw the little red-topped one start walking out into the first lane and from above it looked like Frogger but the frog was red. And he made it past the first line and he made it past the second. But on the third, and final line, he ran into a blue car and the blue car tried to not be run into—but it happened anyway. I heard the red-top-frogger's friends laughing and some weren't laughing and then they ran to get somebody I guess. I just went to work and I looked where the once-red-top-frogger almost made it across and there was more red on the road. The red stretched under the overpass and onto the other side for a ways. I just went to work and when I got there I washed my hands and put on my headset and took the order from the first car in line. I did my shift and then went home to go the hell to bed.

* * *

I think a lot at night when I get home from work.

Like, outside of the box thinking.

The house is normally quiet when I get home and I try my hardest to not wake-up Father or sleeping-Sister. I get into bed and then I'll just think. I like to think. The life meanings, and the 'whatarewedoingheres' creep in but they are only one instrument in the marching band beating around my head.

47

I'm like a kid thinking too hard at night. I start slow. Or I try to. I think beyond my street, and then beyond my state, and into the solar system where I could see the world like how it was in a clay science class diagram or something. And once I get that far out I push the throttle down a bit further and gas off into the universe. I try to edge towards the ends of the galaxy, but no matter what, I can't get into the bigger sphere beyond. It is like a self-induced brain-freeze of sorts; a mind trap that I set, and then step into.

The thought of what is out there.

If we live, here on this earth, and we all know that we are going to die, then when we die we go to heaven or hell, but are not reborn like the people in one steeple say, then we float in heaven or hell forever and there is no dying there, so there is nowhere to go after that and then that means we are stuck there, we can't get out of the place that we're not even sure exists and we have to stay there for all of eternity?

It would be around this time that thinking becomes like punching myself in its own head.

Oh, but after the punching comes petting.

Maggie creeps in.

Maggie normally creeps in to wish me goodnight. She will tell me not to worry about all of that 'bigger stuff' and to just take life "less seriously."

"We are only here for a little time Jakey (she calls me Jakey) we should just love and spend it being happy."

That Maggie. She's got a way to make everything seem like it is bouncing around in a pink skirt, wielding pom-poms and shirts with one big letter on it that fits too tightly.

Imaginary Maggie will sit with her back up against the fence of the tennis court and she will let me sit in front of her in-between her legs. I'll use her for a back rest; something to lean on. And she'll run her fingers through my hair and every now and then when we've slouched she will pull me up under my ribs closer to her like a small child.

48

Imaginary Maggie tells me how happy she is that she has someone to talk to and that she likes me just the way I am.

Just like me. Just plain old Jakey.

But after the self-inflicted-thought-punches and the Imaginary Maggie swoons, I remember Maggie's big strong blonde Richy-Richard boyfriend and roll over on my pillow, glass in my bed pricks my legs a little as I try to finally fall asleep. It's probably like 3 a.m.

Today [the next day] is Cory's birthday and she told me that she would "'love' to spend it with me," even though she didn't want to "ever see me again." I wish people in this world still meant what they were saying when they spit words out of their stupid little mouths. Like how ridiculous the little gerbils sound when they are standing in the lunch-line and they lean into their friends and toss back their silly hair and mutter, "ughhhhhhhh there is literally nothing to eat today, ughhhhh damnnn ittttt."

"*Literally* nothing to eat" poops out of their mouth while they are standing in a line built around the distinct, singular purpose, of delivering them food to put in their fat-little-pink-mouths.

So Cory tells me she would 'love' me to spend the day with her. Like her birthday is a holiday. Like her heart would break into hundreds of pieces if I didn't take her to a Red Robin, or a T.G.I. Fridays for a twenty-dollar meal. Like this day was a dollar bill and we both put our hands on its corners and flattened it out and stuck it in the vending machine to get a drink that would nourish our thirst. The spending of a day only exists if something is supposed to exist in its response.

So I take her to the Ruby Tuesday's on Herndon.

I have the day off from work and after school I could care less what we do really. She gets to feel like a woman or important and I get to avoid going home and playing that game. The game with spacey-Sister where we pretend all that is, isn't, and the game with Father where we really try hard to act like he really tries hard.

At Ruby Tuesdays we don't eat very fast. Cory keeps looking at the dessert menu and she eats her hamburger slow. I just got a cheese burger and I slurp down my Coke drinks one after the other. In between one bite Cory thanks me for sharing her birthday with her. Then after the next bite she wipes her mouth and sets her napkin down and sits up in her chair. She blinks her eyes and then asks me about the other day in the back gymnasium. I just chew on my straw and act like I don't know what she's talking about.

"I just...ya know Jack...If you don't want to try to do that stuff...ya know like...we don't have to ya know...I just heard, like...the other girls talking about all that stuff were supposed to do and, like...I don't know...ya know?!"

I knew what she was talking about. I know all about that 'stuff' she's spitting on and on about but I just get up and go use the bathroom like I didn't hear what she was saying.

Cory is just Cory.

She's not anything more than that and I don't need her to be anything more than that. I can be happy and plenty real being by myself. She's a space-filler, a time-killer, someone to smoke with. She's not Maggie.

After hamburgers Cory orders her birthday-fudge-brownie and sits slowly eating the whole thing. Small-fork by small-fork bite; like if she eats it slower it's more womanly. Like if she eats it slower maybe her body will be fooled about how shitty it is. After she finishes I pay the bill with my hard-ass-work-McDonalds-money and we finally leave. Since it's her birthday, Cory drives her parent's car and she wants to give me a ride home but I want to walk. She goes one way and I leave the other way and walk on the bricks like a tightrope. She yells back goodnight to me but in my head I'm walking miles above some city in between sky-scrapers; I can't hear a Cory from up there.

Tonight when I got home was perfect. It wasn't too late but Father was passed-REMSLEEP-out in his chair with the usual cardboard tearings of a 12-pack of beer scattered around by his feet. I shut the

50

door quietly as I came in, but I probably could have just fucking slammed it.

But that's not what made it perfect!

By the black-bag sitting on the kitchen counter it looks to me like little smart-Sister rented the school laptop and little super-Sister looks to be all done with it.

These were the best nights for me 'cus I could look at stuff that I couldn't look at on the school computers. They got like a Big Brother situation going on with the computer screens where boss-man-at-the-front-desk can see what everybody's looking at and working on and you can't use the computers anymore if you look at raw shit. Like I want to.

Just to be sure I can use it I should probably go upstairs to talk to Sister:

"Sister?!"

"Hey Brother, yeah good Brother?"

"Oh dear, sweet little perfect Sister of mine...I couldn't help but notice the school laptop sitting on the really clean counter downstairs."

"Oh, why yes smart Bother! I rented it from the school library today!"

"How remarkable wise Sister, do you think, if you are finished of course, that a good soul like me may use it for some research and studying and such!?"

"Oh Brother, what is mine is yours you know this! Have a lovely night!"

But it's *way* funnier in my head. So I don't go ask. I just grab the laptop and charger from the bag and go to my room. If she needs it she'll bang on my door.

Step 1) turn on laptop and plug charger into wall

Step 2) steal happy neighbors WiFi

Step 3) pull list of names out from drawer

Step 4) go to Google and type first name: **Albert Fish**

51

Albert Fish (Killings between 1919 and 1930): Albert Fish may have been America's most vile pedophile, serial killer, and cannibal. He is known by many names — Gray Man, Brooklyn Vampire, The Boogeyman, and the Werewolf of Wysteria. He was a gentle-looking and benevolent grandfather, a total contrast to the monster within him. His wife considered him a wonderful husband and his children believed he was a model father. Some of his crimes seem unbelievable.

Background

Hamy Fish (his birth name) was born in Washington D.C. as the youngest of four children. Several of his family members had mental health problems. After his father's death, he was put in an orphanage by his mother and he was whipped at the orphanage frequently. That's said to be when he began to realize that he enjoyed physical pain and felt aroused by it.

Step 5) read results, make notes on list

I have an utter fascination with killers. I don't know why. Maybe the idea that they made such big decisions about life and death and that stuff makes them seem powerful. Maybe I think they are special because they did exactly what they wanted to do exactly how they planned to do it (most of the time at least). Maybe I envy them or maybe I hate them so much that I want to know more about them. Maybe I see myself in them. Like sometimes I see similar struggles or sometimes something that seems the same, like a drunk Dad and no Mom, and it shows me one way people deal with it. I don't know, I couldn't tell you exactly why. But I *love* them. And I mean my words when I say that. I love them because they seem real to me. They don't seem like they would bring home that $20 bottle of wine. They seem like they would break that bottle, and for some reason that feels real; refreshing. That feels like what I would do.

I'll stay up all night working my way down my list of names. I only get to do this when we have the laptop at the house and most of the time I don't even know how long I've been searching. It's like paging through a scrapbook; this is the only way I can possibly try to describe it to someone. I turn the page, and search the next killer, or monster as they call them, and there is this face that belongs to a person I have never met but I feel like I know them, like in the distance. And there are words connected to these floating-heads like; 'motives,' 'background,' 'reasons,' 'history,' that seem like they are talking about me. It is like a normal person taking a walk down scrap-book-memory-lane. They know who is in the pictures and when they see them a certain emotion turns inside of them as they think back to the time or place where or when the pictures or events happened. That turning-inside-me-emotion is the important part. The magical part maybe. But I wish it was more like my yearbook. More like I shared the day with these people and knew them face to face and sat beside them in homeroom. More like that then in distant memory-lane-pictures.

But nonetheless, it keeps me up till 5:30 and it makes sassy-Sister wonder why the laptop is so hot in the morning when she packs it up for school. But I just keep up with my list and its columns; Name, Where From, Motive, Father & Mother?, Method, Weapon, How Many Dead.

I hope that spectacular-Sister brings the laptop back home soon.

I'm pretty sure it is Thursday and that means I have to work tonight; *ughhhhhhhhhhhhhhhhhhhhhhhh*. I'm sitting in first-block and my mind is like a freakin' railroad train. One direction and it's moving, man. All I can think about is last night. The names are popping in and out of my head followed by motives and floating faces of sleeping, leaking victims. Man what they must have been thinking, like how when Richard Trenton Chase cracked those six people with his bullets and then drank their blood. How real. How astonishingly real. Or the night Dennis Rader, with his carefully-planned-killing-packet set out to strangle and tie up his victims until they passed out and then he let them come back up right, and then strangled them again. How incredibly... actual. To see people like that. To see people for what they are in their moments. In their trials, in their panics, in their fears, and in their crying and in their screaming.

Just to see something real, to feel it, to create it.

53

Unlike this fucking English quiz. I turn mine in covered in doodles and eraser marks and pen scratches. This stuff isn't authentic. It's like a time-filler, a space-killer.

As soon as the bell rings I'm up and running out of the English trailer. Our school has overflow so they shuffle us into these trailers for some classes. They're cold and damp and they smell like aluminum and mildew and I'm not in there a minute more than I need to be.

I'm all jazzed up from thinking about last night and my heart is bumpbumpbump-racing. I'm that railroad train still, barreling forward with my backpack slung over one shoulder and bouncing all around. I'm all bumping into people as I slam back into the building and pace as rapidly as possible through the glances and through the hallway to the back gymnasium. Fuck.

Fuck I got to be alone right now.

Forget going to Humphries man, forget Humphries.

I fling down the hallway to the back gymnasium and reach around beneath the small zipper pocket on my backpack.

Yeah, it's still there. New Cardinal Issue, Spyder Tactical knife that I got from Good Ol' Fritzy after I lost my other good one in that loud-dog's loud-throat. *Miss that one but this new ones at least two-inches bigger.* Fritzy stole it from his dad and sold it to me for my hard-fucking-work-golden-archway-money.

So I'm breaking down the hallway carrying sweat on my head and on my arms and on my legs and bumping into the wall like someone else is controlling my legs.

I get right past the boys locker room and keep moving as fast as I can; just silly boys in there, whipping each other with towels or prancing around talking about t-shirts or tennis shoes.

Save them.

Keep going… Girl's locker room.

Stop here.

Feel Cardinal Issue Spyder Tactical knife burning a hole right through my backpack, man, feel it burning up my hand.

54

Look down hallway.

Albert Fish. Dennis Radar. John Haigh. Javed Iqbal. Charles Manson. Ted Bundy. Jeffrey Dahmer. Richard Trenton Chase. Gregory Brazel. Carrol Cole. Terry Blair.

No one in the hallway. Okay, kick open the door, just like always, just like principle Yadayadayadafuckingyada told you not to "a hundred times…"

Then out of nowhere, beautiful long legged Maggie swings the blue door open like she's Kramer or something and her perfect marble eyes are laser-beaming my soul. I get a shock from my legs to my hair and my tongue feels like it's stuck up to a 9-volt.

"Oh, it's *you.* Look I don't think you're supposed to be back here alright you're gonna' get yourself into trouble like last time."

Fucking LONG LEG MAGGIE! My nighttime companion, my fictional flower, my hope, sharing glances and words with me like were ol' pals and I'm standing here with my jaw on the floor. I don't say anything.

I sling the other shoulder-strap of my backpack up over my other shoulder and wipe the sweat from my head is what I do. Then I walk my ass back to class. I walk slow and look at the picture sitting behind my eyes. The picture of Maggie is there and it's bright and prominent. Eyes like a flashlight. She's in my head but she seems so real.

And that was my week, man. I mean it's like I said; "I am normal and tall and I haven't brought my clothes to dress-out for gym since like three weeks ago." I mean it's pretty accurate, pretty troubled just like every kid growing up, ya know. Everybody's dealing with something.

Oh yeah, like this kid from our rival High School down the county a-ways. They hung up the paper clipping in the cafeteria and there was an announcement in homeroom this morning about it. Some sixteen-year-old 'yupp was in the cafeteria in the morning with everybody before class and he had a gun in his backpack. They said it was his Dad's gun; legally owned. The boy was like super-smart; had a 3.8 GPA and was captain of like every team. They said he dates a beautiful girl with long legs and big eyes from one of the close by high schools. His parents are still together and his Mom calls him 'Johnny'. But anyway he pulled out that gun in the middle of the morning announcements and pulled the-go-button like five times in the direction of his teacher. He killed him. Now the world will hear about it like it did the cop who got shot here. And the President will board Air Force One and scurry across the nation as quick as he can. And he will release a formal statement with some 'jibberbjabber' and then give a speech in the school's auditorium. Something about "now more than ever," or "rise like a Pheonix." There won't be a dry eye in the house. The press will fill their tummies, and Jonny's parents will tell them all how good their boy was, and how he would never do something this monstrous.

In a Ghost City, a Crosswalk Signal Chirps

driveways stop after a few feet and turn
into lawns turned into forest

Around the perimeter of town
a highway is empty
a crack splitting it wider each day
Kids peer inside, leave
tennis shoes lining the crack
in minutes, come back to melted rubber

There are some who say
there is no permanence to what we do
but 300 feet below
a vein of coal has burned for 100 years

Plumes of smoke seep out of earth
stream around the old cemetery
meet with fog on a cloudy day

The Macbeth Tree

Tallahatchie County, Mississippi

Lightning-struck
and prematurely twisted
in the middle of fallow land
with no camouflage
stands a Devil's bargain,
its knobbed and threadbare
branches reaching up
a plea for deliverance.

Naked and black-burnt
lesson in deformed
humility, with no safe
surface to carve initials
in a heart or rest a weary
back, these witch
branches left to smolder
in an open field,
a silent prayer of witness,
thin as a hag's finger,
warning the sky.

More Or Less About Rachel

Ulrike, crossing the traffic circle, on the way to a meeting at the School of Communication (where she was adjunct) marveled, as she often did, at how the swirling cars and pedestrians managed, almost always, not to collide. The world was full of subtle, unnoticed choreography. Performers almost slamming into each other but—last second—veering away.

Constant, brilliant improv.

She entered the park. It was a mild November; she walked under half-bare trees, holding her coffee, which slowly cooled, while the planet seemed to do the opposite. From somewhere she heard Blondie. Still, occasionally, as if out of nostalgia, someone brought a boom box to the park. It was not surprising to Ulrike that, hearing this, she thought of Rachel. People had their associations. Rachel had been her friend once, on the opposite coast, in the last century. Once, at Cafe Tuzzi, not far from the bay, Ulrike had told Rachel about a problem. The problem, at the time, had seemed immense to Ulrike. Intractable; deep pain. Now, crossing the park, patchy grass, gray squirrels, the problem seemed a distant nothing. Like the wisps of clouds above the School of Communication, the brown monolith on the park's far side. But Ulrike could still remember Rachel's response. Or, really, her reaction to it. Rachel (in Cafe Tuzzi) had told her about an experience *she'd* had which Rachel thought was similar. This had irked Ulrike (so much more labile then). She'd thought, then, in the last century, in the cafe, that Rachel's experience *wasn't* like her own. *Hardly*. Hers had been painful and significant. Complex in a way that Rachel, dressed in black, probably, wearing her orange and green scarf, possibly, and some cool earrings, surely, clearly had not comprehended. She'd known what Rachel was trying to do. She thought she was "mirroring" Ulrike's experience. A particular subspecies of "mirroring" in which, to show understanding, one offered an experience similar to the one described. But the parallel experience Rachel had proffered hadn't, Ulrike had felt, been parallel at all. She'd gone over this in her head, as it tossed on her pillow, in her attic apartment, deep into the night, on a hill not far from the foggy bay. She'd listed all the reasons *her* experience wasn't like Rachel's. Rachel had, Ulrike had thought (in the last century), been trying to make it *about herself.* These were of course thoughts in context; Ulrike had evidence, or believed she had, that Rachel often tried to make things about herself. What had puzzled Ulrike then, and puzzled her now, clutching her coffee, crossing the gray park, where the squirrels darted and the people sat or ambled, was that, sometimes, it seemed entirely right (according to Ulrike's surely never to be published general theory of communication) to do just what Rachel had seemed to think she *was* doing: offering-an-account-of-an-experience-more-or-less-parallel-to-the-one-about-which-you-are-being-told. Had it been that she'd gone so *immediately* to her own experience, without expending sufficient attention to the details of Ulrike's? Would it have been better if the parallel had seemed, to Ulrike, *more* parallel? There might be a parallel universe, there might be many, thought Ulrike, in the park, as the birds flew, in coordination, overhead. But each person was a universe, and they weren't parallel. They often crashed. Or far more often, in her world at least, just averted it. The city was full of aversions. The world was.

The sky changed like a mood. Ulrike clutched her coffee. Smell of chestnuts. Holidays coming. And Rachel would be where? Ulrike knew she *may* have been unfair, long ago, at the cafe. How was one to know whether the experience you offered, your proffered parallel, really *was* parallel? Had it been fair of her to expect such knowledge from Rachel? Ulrike knew she often did not know whether the experiences *she* offered as parallels were indeed similar to the ones being shared. She went on intuition. Sometimes she got it wrong. Often she became irked

60

when her parallel was rejected, when she, Ulrike, was told no, it really wasn't the same, as had happened with her friend Luis the week before. She'd gotten angry at Luis in the way one does when a gift is not accepted graciously. She'd hidden her anger from herself and him, bundling it as she might have wrapped herself against the wind if it were colder. Pride was shit; it went before the fall or was the fall, and it was everywhere. Oh, clichés. They too were everywhere. Rachel probably would have gotten angry at her if, outright, rather than furtively, on that afternoon in Cafe Tuzzi, in the last century, Ulrike had rejected the parallel rather than just brooding about it, in her attic, in the foggy nights, near the bay. Of course Rachel, who'd been her best-friend-maybe then, had probably sensed that Ulrike hadn't been impressed—if not in that instance, then in others, in other conversations, in other cafes. And if not in the moment, then sometime later. Hurt, Ulrike knew, often worked that way. It came back to you as if on a delay, the way that on television there was a pause between live and seen—to screen for obscenity. A student read on a green bench. A man, likely homeless, snoozed. Words weren't the only means of communication; there was the vast nonverbal world. Expressions, gestures, inflections subtle as the weak and shifting wind.

Rachel was gone from her life now. But from Rachel had come her friendship with Luis. One might say life was funny that way. But it wasn't, Ulrike thought. Funny. Many things made her laugh, but not the way people moved apart. She was lost in all this as she crossed the park. A squirrel ran in front of her. She almost tripped over the squirrel. Some of her coffee spilled, but luckily not on the squirrel. She and the squirrel looked at each other. This was not supposed to happen. People weren't supposed to trip over squirrels. They both seemed embarrassed, almost awkward. Ulrike knew, or believed, that this couldn't be so. It seemed a good bet that squirrels did not feel social awkwardness: experience once again not matching science. How odd, she thought, that she remembered so clearly that moment—or, really, its aftermath—that stuff between her and Rachel, which had all occurred, one could say, if one wished, so long ago.

Disclaimer for Disney's Pinocchio: February 1940

There will be colors, shapes and Italy.
For a while, at least,
all will go horribly wrong.

The floors will be sticky.
The cricket will sing.
You will like his songs.

If a stranger invites you
through the screen,
into this dream village

where the voices of animals
invite you to stroke their soft fur
then warm your hands

in their mouths,
run home.
If nothing in the theater

threatens you,
know, at least, that you will
leave a changed girl.

You will walk home down
Saginaw Street with a little piece

of yourself dissolving
in the belly of that whale.
In Stromboli's cage another bit
will wait to sing and dance

for strange men
and women and children
who were never warned

that your orphan song
will forever change them.
I will be listening.

Though I will like your song
and wish you the best,
I will not be able to save you.

The Boy

They had gathered on the front lawn. Four of them. Howard only recognized two—Tom Riordan and Jimmy O'Toole, the boy's oldest friends. It had been snowing earlier, but the snow had turned to rain, the yard to slush. Mud. The yard looked filthy, everything looked filthy. Winter was nearly over, leaving melting brown and gray snow banks, soiled with exhaust, in its wake, and it had been the longest winter Howard could remember in some time. Howard and his family lived on the corner of the busiest street in Willington, traffic at all hours, and this time of day the trucks never seemed to stop coming. Loud in the wet, and then roaring, speeding, away. The kids had been out there for a while, shouting at the house, shouting "Chickie", shouting for the boy, and after listening to them for what seemed an eternity, Howard had gone out, his wife Barbara at his side, and brokered a deal. A fight.

It was 1982.

The boy had been refusing to go to school. He cried each morning as Howard dragged him to the car, and then he cried again when he returned home at the end of the day. Eighth grade, almost fourteen. He had never been a problem before, never been a bad boy—he could be fresh at times but it was never something that a quick back hand couldn't immediately correct—and he had always been popular. Ever since pre-school. He had started skating, playing hockey, at three, and there were always plenty of kids to meet at the rink. He was a skillful hockey player, and a tough one, a defenseman never one to shy from a fight—a good fighter on the ice—and that was made everything that was happening all the more perplexing. He no longer had any friends, not Riordan, not O'Toole. No came by, no one called.

They all hate me, he finally confessed, and they tortured him. Is that what you want? he had asked Howard. To see people torture me? He was sitting at the kitchen table, his head down, his yellow and green, wool, Snoopy hat pulled down tight over his ears, and still bundled in his black and gold Boston Bruins jacket. A bit of snot dripping from his nose.

Howard hesitated a moment. He could smack him again, but he wasn't convinced that, at this point, it would do any good. "No," Howard said. "I want you to stand up for yourself."

"I can't," the boy said. "That's what I keep telling you. I can't do it any more. I've tried."

Chickie. They were calling him "Chickie," short for "chicken." He said they chanted it in the locker room, in the cafeteria, they sent him nasty notes, and drew pictures of him on the blackboard. And if the weaker boys, and girls, didn't tease him, too, they were threatened with the same treatment. So they all complied. Better him, than them, Howard imagined they figured, and some of them had already been getting it for years. The boy, had not. Up until this point, Howard was fairly sure, the boy had been one of the ones giving it. It was nothing to be proud of, but it was better than this. Anything was better than this. Watching your child suffer was unbearable enough, but when you didn't know why, it just made it worse. The feeling of helplessness gnawing daily at your belly.

Howard was a big man, enormously over weight. He needed to place a pad between the steering wheel and his belly in order to slide into the car and operate the wheel, and this had always made the boy laugh. He thought it was the funniest thing he had ever seen, and despite the subject matter, Howard enjoyed making him laugh. Other than obvious concerns for his health, his weight didn't bother him much. He was happily married with a beautiful home and a good business, and there wasn't much more that he needed from life. He hadn't always been fat, hadn't always been different, and so he hadn't been subject to the ridicule his son was experiencing when he himself

66

was in school. He, too, had played hockey, a high school star, and he almost made it to the minors. The Boston Braves. Several scouts had come looking at him, but in the end, he didn't have enough speed, and it hadn't worked out. He was close to thirty when the pounds started piling on, and then just kept piling, but he had always carried himself in way where it didn't matter. He wasn't just a fat guy—he meant business and he called the shots. Now he owned a share of a semi pro team that came out of Lynn, and a small advertising company right in the center of town. Barbara, his wife, golfed with him on Saturdays, and she manned the home the rest of the week. The house was spotless. Always. Dishes weren't allowed out of the kitchen, and toys weren't allowed out of the attic and the cellar. Not in the bedrooms, not in the halls. Barbara chain smoked, but she kept it to the kitchen, to keep the nicotine stains off the walls, and she liked scotch after dinner, but she was a good wife, if not the most comely, and she kept one step ahead of all the household affairs. But she, too, couldn't quite understand what was going on with the boy.

"It's like he completely changed overnight," she had said to Howard as he sat at the table one day, sipping his coffee. The kitchen gleamed, it always gleamed. Everything bright white or stainless steel. Not a spot anywhere, and a visitor might wonder if they ever even cooked. Howard's mother had never been much of a housekeeper, and it was one of the things that drew him to Barbara—anything less than immaculate was completely unacceptable. Even the boy. The boy never seemed to be dirty. His clothes never stained nor torn, everything looking new, fresh off the shelf. "He always had an edge," Barbara said. "A confidence about him. And now it's gone." She lit a cigarette. "I can't explain it."

Now, she was at the bottom of the stairs, calling up to the boy, Kyle, demanding he come down. He was hiding in the attic, trying to get as far away as possible from everything that was happening. Barbara yelled that if he didn't come down, she was coming up, and if she had to drag him out herself, it was just going to make it worse. He was

67

going to look like a coward, she yelled, chin raised and one hand on her hip. Is that what he wanted to look like? A coward?

One of the kids out front was now lying down in the snow—the one who had been doing most of the yelling, a kid with sunken, dark eyes who looked like a little Sylvester Stallone—and Howard had to wonder what he was on. He didn't think he was drunk as Howard hadn't smelled alcohol when he had gone out there, and Howard himself didn't drink, so if any of them were drinking, he would have smelled it. If they were drinking, he would have called it all off. You never knew what people were capable of when drinking, and Howard wanted a clean fight.

The plan was for the boy to fight Riordan. Howard and Barbara had dared him, dared all of them. One of them. They had told them that they were all spineless, that not one of them had to the guts to take the boy on alone because they knew he would win. And what would happen then? Howard had asked. What would happen if he won?

Howard had earlier contemplated just calling the cops, but in the long run, that wouldn't have made things any better. The boy still had to go back to school, and if he called the cops on them, these kids weren't going to forget it—the whole school wouldn't forget it, the boy just looking all the more the chicken—so in the end they made the deal. Riordan would fight the boy, and if the boy won, they would stop. They would leave him alone. They would get the whole school to leave him alone. The Riordan kid looked nervous for a second, scared and second guessing himself—if the boy did beat him, *he* would never hear the end of it —but then he had agreed. He had to agree. He had been dared to fight the boy, and how could he ever face his friends if he backed down? But Howard couldn't care less about how he would face his friends. He only cared about the boy, and he knew the boy would win. That would finish it. It would be over.

Now Howard pulled back the curtain. Barbara was still staring up the stairs, a stare intense enough, hot enough, to melt wax. The boy himself had always had a temper, and he had gotten it from Barbara.

68

She had told Howard and the boy, told the boys outside, that when she was young, she had bad skin and the kids, boys and girls, used to pick on her. And when they picked on her, she said, she used to beat the crap out of them. And Howard believed she probably had. Barbara was perpetually red in the face, and her eyes were steely blue. Eyes that would probably be beautiful, Howard had always figured if they were ever at ease. But they were not. Never. Outside on the lawn he could almost see the steam coming off her in the cold air. She was right up there, right in the boys' faces, and Howard thought for a moment, she might just haul off and hit one of them herself.

"Look at you all," she said, "stoned out of your minds, and he's Chickie? Is that why he's Chickie? Because he won't do drugs and pick on kids weaker than he is?"

"That has nothing to do with it," the Riordan kid said. "He used to pick on more kids than any of us."

"Nothing to do with it?" Barbara yelled. "Nothing to do with it? Then what the hell is it?"

Riordan swallowed his breath. "His skin," he said.

"His skin?" Barbara yelled. "What the hell does bad skin have to do with being a chicken?"

The little, one, straggly hair, who looked like a mouse, smiled. "Pock," he said. "Pock, pock, pock."

* * *

It had all started nearly three months back. Just after Christmas. The boy had come home upset, saying he had gotten into a fight, an argument, with Tom Riordan, said he was being a jerk—but neither Barbara nor Howard thought much of it at the time. Kids fought. That's what they did. And nine times out of ten they would have made up an hour or two, or at best a day, later. But it didn't happen. A week went past, then two. And then the boy confessed it was because of his skin.

His skin. The boy looked like his mother—at least like the pictures Howard had seen of her when she was a girl—and he had always

69

seemed to blend right in. He wasn't a looker, but he wasn't ugly—dirty blond hair and a lot of freckles and the same blue eyes—but then about six months back, well before the trouble all started, his skin had begun to break out. So quickly and so dramatically, it was shocking.

Howard had never seen anything like it. The boy's face literally erupted. Mountains of acne that just wouldn't move. Lumps and welts. It was as if he had tectonic plates shifting beneath the surface. It was painful just to look at it. He and Barbara had immediately taken him to see a dermatologist but nothing seemed to work. Not prescriptions. Creams and pills and needles. "It might just be something he has to ride out," the doctor had said. "Hormones. The blood. He's changing. We can probably make it a little better, but I don't think it's going to go away until he's out of adolescence. The boy had asked when that would be, and the doctor shot him an estimate, and then the boy started to cry. Barbara had told him on the way home, that she had gone through the same thing as a teenager, that it didn't last forever, and then the boy had snapped at her, blaming her. People were talking about it, he said. They pointed at him, said things when they didn't think he was listening.

"Well, smack them then," Howard had said from behind the wheel.

The boy sniffled. "Next time, I probably will."

But that was then. He wasn't making threats to smack anyone anymore. And along with "Chickie," the children had also made up other nicknames for him. *Pizza face. Scurf Turf. H.R. Pus and Stuff.* But to Howard, it still didn't make much sense. Plenty of kids, both popular and unpopular, had bad skin, and it didn't necessarily make them pariahs. It was part of life. Growing up. Obstacles, challenges help define character he heard himself telling the boy one day on the way to the skating rink. You learn from then, overcome them, and then in the long run they make you a better man. Look at Job.

"I don't know who that is," the boy had said.

Howard cleared his throat. "He was in the Bible. A guy in the Bible."

70

"I bet he didn't have skin that looked like this," said the boy.

"His skin looked even worse," Howard said, and as soon as he did, he wondered if it were true. If he had read that. He tried to remember. "God made him a leper. Leprosy. You know what that is?"

"Yes," he said. "You're skin falls off."

"Well, you see? That's even worse."

"No, it's not."

"It's not?"

"No. Because if my skin fell off I wouldn't have all these zits."

The boy took some of his frustrations/aggressions out in the rink, and Howard liked to watch him practice. He could check and he could shove, and still, occasionally during games he could take off the gloves and come to blows. Quick fights before the ref would blow the whistles. The kids he was slugging were from different towns, and innocent in his persecution, but somebody, somehow, had to answer, Howard figured. That's the way the world had always been. Howard, a hot pretzel in hand, wondered why it had to end once he left the ice.

"If you clock Tommy Riordan like that, the way you did that kid from Norwell," he said one day on the way home, "I don't think he'll be calling you names anymore."

"If I clock Tommy Riordan like that," the boy said, "they'll be about ten kids behind him ready to jump on me."

* * *

Now, Barbara had headed up to the attic. Michelle, their daughter, came out after she did. Michelle had been in the kitchen, doing her homework. She was a good student and always did her homework immediately upon getting home. Before everything started, the boy would do his homework right away, right there beside her, and then go off with his friends. Now, more often than not, he just sat there. Not touching his pencils, not touching the paper, looking to be in a daze. His grades were dropping, everything was dropping, and the disruption in the homework routine was just one of many. Their lives had had order—Howard liked order—and now it was just one big disruption.

71

Howard looked at his daughter. She looked worried. More scared than sad, maybe about to cry herself. If she had been in his school, she would have something to say to them, to all of them, she had told Howard, but she wasn't. Michelle was three years older than the boy, and she had some problems with her skin, but nothing as bad as his, and besides, Howard thought, it wouldn't have mattered much if she did. Michelle wasn't unpopular, but she wasn't popular either. She was just another kid. You couldn't fall too far when you've never been very high. The boy had been high. Howard was sure of it.

"He still up there?" Michelle asked him.

Howard just looked back out the window. The kid who had passed out had gotten up and left, stumbled off down the street, but the others were still there. Waiting.

"Someone has to get him down," he said at last. "I'm sick of it. I want this over with. I want it over with today. This ends today."

Barbara, upstairs, had started to scream. The boy shouting back. He wasn't coming down, wasn't going to go out there. There was some banging then. Footsteps on the floor. Howard's heart picked up, his belly growling. Whenever he got angry, his belly began to growl.

"If she kills him, he's not going to be able to fight anybody," Michelle said.

Howard went to the bottom of the stairs himself now. He didn't want to climb them. Not three flights up. Three flights, and he'd be resting for ten minutes. He'd lose his poise, and that wouldn't do anyone any good. Not right now.

"Kyle!" he shouted. "Now!"

* * *

They had called the school, been to see the principal. The principal was a big man with a bald head who wore short sleeve dress shirts in the middle of the winter. His nose twisted slightly to the left, and he had black and white photographs of a younger version of himself sparring in boxing shorts and gloves adorning his office. He noticed Howard looking at the photographs. "I keep them up there for the

72

kids," he said with a short laugh. "They get a kick out of it, and it doesn't hurt to put the fear of God in them."

"God being?" Howard asked.

The principal leaned back, raised his eyebrows a bit. "I could have been a contender, Charlie."

Howard hesitated, unsure how to respond.

"I'm joking," the man said. "Just joking. I did okay, but it was all amateur stuff. Then I figured it was better to use my brain than have it beaten and compressed. Just the same, I wish the school committee would still allow a little intramural boxing—with appropriate head gear of course—in the school here. They won't of course, not these days, but they used to, and it was a good way for kids to get out their frustrations. Build some confidence. Something like that might be just the thing your son needs to get back on track. Just my opinion, off the record of course."

"Or you could discipline some of the kids who are tormenting him," Howard said. Barbara was just staring at the man. She hadn't said a word.

"If we catch them, we will," the man said. "I promise you that. The tough part is catching them. Kids are so sneaky these days—they're not going to do anything, say anything, when the teacher is looking."

"But Kyle says it's the whole school," Howard says. "Everybody."

The man sighed. "And it may well be. It's a vicious age. No doubt about that. They're all starting puberty, changing, and all pretty unsure about themselves. Insecure. And insecurity breeds contempt. It brings out the worst in a lot of people, not just kids. When somebody is feeling bad about themselves, there's nothing better than making someone else feel worse. The failures of others makes them feel better about themselves."

"I don't see how having bad skin can be considered a failure," Howard said.

73

"No, of course not," said the man. "But that doesn't mean kids don't view it that way." He hesitated a moment, staring at Howard. "They look at physical imperfections as weaknesses. One in the same."

The principal had sent his secretary to pull the boy from class, and the boy looked mortified upon his arrival, seeing Howard and Barbara sitting there in the office. Howard hadn't told him they were coming, wanted it to be a surprise. If he knew that they really were in his corner, he figured, if he could see that first hand, see that they were circling the wagons, it may help turn this thing around, it may help build his confidence. Instead he looked as if he were about to cry again.

The principal didn't sit back down behind his desk, he stood in front of it. Arms folded, forearms bulging. He had the fading tattoo of an anchor on one of them. The Navy insignia. He gave the boy his spiel, explained why Howard and Barbara were there, and then he began with his line of questioning. Who, when, and where? Why?

The boy just looked at him, not answering at first.

"We can't help if we don't know," the man said.

"It's not a big deal," the boy said at last. "I think it was just a misunderstanding."

The man cocked his head a little. "Your parents seem to think it's more than that. They seem to think it's a very big deal."

"It's not," said the boy. "I just don't get along with a couple of kids that all."

Howard swallowed his breath. "You need to tell him the truth."

"I am," said the boy.

"That's not what you told us," Howard snapped. On a certain level he was afraid this might happen, but even still he wasn't prepared. "Tell him what you've been telling us."

"I've just been telling you that to make you feel bad," the boy said. "So I wouldn't have to go to school."

"Well, why don't you want to come to school?" asked the principal. "You're a good student."

"I don't know."

74

"Well, there must be a reason," said the man.

"I just want to watch cartoons," said the boy.

* * *

The principal had walked them to the door, assuring them he would pull aside three or four of the boys they mentioned—*have a little chat with them*, he said—and who knew, maybe if they stopped the others would, too. That's what it was all about, he said, the whole world. Leaders and followers.

They asked the principal if they could have the boy dismissed for the day, and then they lit into him as soon as they reached the car. How could he have made fools of them like that? Here they were going to bat for him, sticking their necks out for him, and he turned around and stabbed them in the back. How?

"So, what's the real story?" Barbara demanded. "Are the picking on you or not?"

Howard pulled away from the curb, looked at the boy in the rear view. The boy was huddled against the door, staring out the window. He was looking smaller and smaller each day. He wasn't growing, getting bigger, he was getting smaller. Howard knew it wasn't possible, but that was how it seemed. He had started crying again. The crying never seemed to end. And with a girl it was one thing—girls were supposed to cry—but with a boy, after a certain age, too much was too much. You had to turn things around.

"You should have told me you were coming to the school," he said. "Then I could have just taken off, I could've run away. Now you've just made it worse."

"How the hell could we have made it worse?" Howard asked. "We talked to Mr. Janowsky and now he's going to look into it. You can't tell me those kids are going to keep up the bullshit if a guy like that tells them to knock it off."

"They don't care what he says," said the boy. "They don't care about anything. And now kids saw you and it's going to be all over the school. You're already like a legend as it is, and now tons of more kids are going to have seen you."

Howard scowled. "A legend? For what?"

"Nothing," he said quietly.

"Your father asked you question, Kyle," said Barbara, "and you better answer him."

"Because they make fun of you, too," whispered the boy.

"Me?" Howard asked. "What do they make fun of me for?"

Kyle had his face pressed against the glass. "Because you're so fat."

* * *

When they got home, Howard had stepped on the scale. Kyle had gone to his room, pulled the blankets over his head, and Barbara was down in the kitchen. Smoking and scrubbing. Scrubbing at spots on the counter that had disappeared months, years before. The house was so quiet this time of the day in the middle of winter. The world was so quiet. He could hear the muffled voices of men on the radio—news radio—coming from the downstairs in the kitchen, but that was all. Another time of day, the voices would never have made it up here. He sucked in his belly and leaned forward to look down at his toes. Three sixty-five.

When had he gotten so big? It didn't seem completely gradual—going up a couple sizes every year or so—but it didn't seem to happen overnight either. Barbara had always said it didn't bother her, so if it didn't bother her, it didn't bother him. Not as much as it could have. No one looked at him any differently. Not that he noticed. And he would notice, he was sure of it. He noticed everything. He remembered fat kids in school. Always placed in the center of the class picture, always picked last in gym. He remembered the nicknames, the laughing. He remembered once in high school gym class they had got hold of one's underwear. They had hung it in the shower room, stretched from the nozzle of one shower to the other. He remembered the boy struggling in the corner to pull back on his shorts. Nothing on beneath; they had wrestled them off him.

76

Howard stepped off the scale and clicked off the light. Mixed with the voices of the radio, he thought he could hear the boy in the room next door. Talking to himself, playing with his soldiers. He was almost fourteen and he still played with soldiers.

* * *

Now he came down the stairs. Just behind Barbara. Barbara marched off to the mudroom to retrieve his coat and gloves and Snoopy hat, but the boy, still sniffling, said he didn't want the gloves—punches didn't hurt as much when you wore gloves, and the other kid could pull the hat down over his eyes, pull it down and keep hitting him. He buttoned his coat, and then wiped his sleeve over his eyes, his nose. "I don't want to do this," he said. "Please."

Barbara was struggling not to shout, but even when she tried not to shout, her voice still carried. It always carried. He would be called a sissy, she was saying, on top of Chickie, they would call him a sissy. Is that what he wanted, to be called a sissy?

"Think of it as just like a game," Howard said to him. "Pretend you're in a game. You're never afraid to get into a fight when you're in a game."

"Please," the boy said one last time, and then Barbara stepped past Howard and pushed open the door. Howard was still holding the hat as the boy started down the walkway.

* * *

After the visit to the principal, getting him to school just became harder. They had talked about sending him to private, but it was a lot of money, and hard to do in the middle of the year. And besides, they had agreed, that was just running away from everything. What good would it do in the long run to run away from everything? The boy started spending more and more time in the attic. His little radio playing. Howard could hear *Aerosmith* playing over and over up there. He knew the album, the cassette tape, because he had bought it for him the year before on his birthday. *Night in the Ruts*. It had been on sale in

77

the discount bin at Kmart. $1.99. The boy liked to listen to it, too. The remake of that old song, "Walkin in the Sand." Over and over.

They had taken him on a visit to a psychiatrist, and the man had suggested trying some medication for depression, but that didn't make any sense. The boy wasn't sick. They knew why he was depressed, he was being tortured.

"How is his diet?" the man had asked, the boy out in the waiting room. The psychiatrist was a small man with thick glasses and dark hair, combed over to the side and coming a bit disheveled. When he smiled he kept his teeth clenched and spread his lips wide as if he were about to receive a polishing from the dentist. He sat with his legs crossed, his legal pad on his knee. He kept photographs throughout his office. A younger picture of himself and his wife, tux and gown, a wedding photo. A blown up studio portrait, the man, his wife and three children, one with the family, goggles on top of their heads, posing on a ski slope, and one of the man in a crowd. Shorts and tank top and number, head back in both victory and agony. Arms raised as he crossed a finish line.

"His diet?" Howard asked, folding his arms over his belly. "His diet is fine. What the hell does his diet have to do with anything?"

The man hesitated. "Well, a lot of people believe that diet has to do with everything. It certainly could be affecting his skin—and from what you tell me, most of his problems began when his skin started to break out—and later in life he could struggle with his weight, just compounding everything. If his self-esteem is as low as it seems to be, problems with his weight would certainly only make things worse."

"He doesn't have any problems with his weight," Howard snapped.

The man paused again. "Of course, not now. But down the line…"

The visits had ended after that. The boy had refused to go back, saying people would just pick on him more if they had found out he was seeing a shrink. Both Barbara and Howard had told him that there was no way anyone would find out, but he still refused, and neither

78

Barbara nor Howard had pushed it. They had spoken with the doctor when they called to cancel, and the man had suggested they give it a little time and try again. In the meantime, he said, it was important to keep a close eye on the boy. Make sure he was safe.

"Well, we know he's not safe," Barbara had said. "That's what this is all about. The other kids won't leave him alone."

"I didn't mean from them," the doctor had said. "I meant from himself."

Howard thought about it for a while after that, but they never brought it up again. The doctor was speaking the impossible. Hurting himself? Other kids maybe, but not his. Not the boy. He had always had an edge. A confidence bordering on arrogance. And it may be gone now, but it would be back. It would have to be back. This whole thing was a phase. One of life's trials. You'll get through this and come out stronger, better, he said. It's temporary. Temporary, he kept telling himself, telling the boy. The biggest lesson I've learned in life, he said, is everything is temporary.

Now, out on the lawn, the boy got in the first shot. A blow to the jaw. Riordan seemed to be in the middle of speaking when the boy clocked him. He staggered a little, and the boy kept coming, but then Riordan ducked, the boy's fist flying over his head, and Riordan got him with a blow to the ribs. The others were jumping about yelling, faces frozen in exhilaration. One called out to watch out for the pus. When his fist connected with his face it was going to splatter the pus. Riordan got underneath him, raising the boy up on his shoulder before tackling him to the ground, the boy pummeling his back with a flurry of fists as he did. They began to roll about the lawn, the slush and the mud, and the boy clawed at Riordan's face, caught his hat and pulled it over his eyes. One of the other's jumped forward and pulled the hat off though before the boy could do any damage, and the Riordan kid put a knee on boy's chest as he raised a fist to connect with his cheek. The boy threw his weight then and got him off him. He started to kick at

79

him, both of them still on the ground, and the others began to chant. Calling him a faggot.

Howard stood frozen at the window beside the door. He pushed his tongue up against the roof of his mouth. Michelle had run upstairs, saying she couldn't watch, but Barbara was still beside him, her shoulder pressed against him. The smell of her perfume was suddenly stronger, mixed with the smell of cigarettes, nicotine, and somewhere beneath the faint smell of scotch.

Howard thought of the kid from the locker room. Things had just gotten worse after that day they had stolen his underwear. A picture spray painted of him on the wall outside the gymnasium, an episode in the cafeteria where he was forced to climb into the trash barrel, covering himself with trash. And then it all culminated when the boy was accused of getting an erection in the shower. Only one other kid had apparently witnessed it, a kid with bad skin and bad breath who spent his life on the fringes himself, but the word quickly got around, finally landing at the feet of the center of their football team. Moose. Moose got hold of the fat boy in the center stair well and beat him black and blue and senseless. Finishing off by kicking him down the stairs, blood dripping from his nose and teeth, and landing unconscious. Howard could remember the students, lining the stairs, the girls with their books pressed against their chests, and the boy lying very still on the floor far below. And where were the teachers? Howard tried to remember. Where was anybody?

Now both Riordan and the boy were on their feet, but Riordan had grabbed the boy by the shoulders and begun kneeing him in the face. The boy turned his head sideways, taking a blow to the temple, and it was the first time since the fight began that Howard got a look at his face. He had his eyes shut tight, trying not to cry, his mouth frozen in pain. Defeat.

Riordan lifted the boy's head and punched him again. The boy stumbled backwards, slipped, landing on his ass, and then the others were laughing. Howard could feel everything building inside him then.

Every day of the past three months. Building and ready to burst. Stealing his breath. One of the kids, the one that looked like a mouse, ran over and kicked the boy. Just in the upper arm, but enough to send the boy slipping further, now flat on his back, holding the arm. And then Jimmy O'Toole took a shot. And then Howard was out the door.

He ran down the walkway, moving full speed, the slush splattering beneath his feet. He had his arms pumping, his legs going as high as he could raise them. He had a flash of a memory. Another day, a warmer day a few years earlier, where he went running across the yard much as he was now. The boy had been with the Tommy Riordan, and the Jimmy O'Toole kid, out in the back yard. Playing, having fun. They had been jumping from a tree into a leaf pile they had raked. Howard was at the door, bringing in the mail, and the boy had called out to him, hand cupped around his mouth. He called him "Tubby Boy!" And then he started to run. He could call him this in fun, and he knew Howard wouldn't mind. It was all in fun. Howard hesitated a moment, and then he decided to run, too, to chase him, have some fun. The other boys saw him coming, arms pumping, and their mouths dropped before they started laughing. It must have been a sight, seeing him in full sprint, but the laughing made it worth it. The boy had jumped into the leaf pile, and then Howard was in there, too, rolling about, playfully whacking the back of the boy's head.

Now none of them were laughing. The other boys saw Howard coming, the look on his face, and they immediately scattered. The small one actually sprinting out across the main street, almost getting hit by a truck. A horn blaring. Howard kept coming though. Too much momentum, he couldn't stop. He passed the boy lying in the slush and the mud, the land sloping down to the street, and as he reached the corner of his yard, his property, he hit a patch of ice and his feet went out from under him. He tried to break his fall with his hands, his elbow, but he came down hard on his back. He could immediately feel the wet and the cold, the mixture of soft slush and hard ice, dead grass and mud, seeping into his clothes, and then he was staring at the sky.

Gray and spitting freezing rain. Howard winced. He could hear the traffic passing on the main street, everything suddenly loud, and he wondered how he looked there, a man his size, lying flat out on the lawn. He turned his head. The other kids were gone. Everyone might has well have been gone except for him and the boy, now sitting up, covered in mud and his face streaked with tears.

Howard rolled over, and tried to climb to his feet and go to him, but the lawn was too slippery, and everything hurt. He had done something to his leg. He looked again at the boy. He tried one more time to get up, his feet slipping out from behind him, and then he clutched the ice in his hands and started to crawl.

Standing at the Intersection of Critical Mass and Event Horizon with Tom Wayne and John Deuser, 5:47 AM

(Or, Hey Man, Is That an Accordian I'm Hearing?)

A million fish wash up dead
in a California harbor.

10, 000 cows keel over in Vietnam.

Thousands of Starlings, Turtle Doves
and Red Wing Blackbirds drop from the sky
in Italy, Sweden, South Dakota.

But elsewheres (and despite it all),
we've still managed to put in
another long (and more than respectable) night
of consorting with spirits and keeping
the Universal Kundalini humming
at that slightly heightened pitch (of radians
per reciprocal seconds) which has been
rumored to induce an "informed
euphoria" of sorts.

And now the early morning streets
(here in mid-town KC/MO, 5:47 AM)
are strangely Frisco/Portland-foggy and deserted
like one of those old-school/bad dream/
where-did-everybody-go sci/fi movies

from our paranoid, cold-war era past.

Or so it would seem
if not for the all-night diner with its
purple neon *OPEN* sign in the window
and the street light on the corner;
a peach-tinted glow hovering above us
like a stationary UFO whose (only mildly
bemused) occupants are, no-doubt, wondering
if these three zombified monkey-boys
and their fucked up little planet
are even worth the effort.

And from somewhere
deep inside the fog,

a strangely musical

wheezing...

Application

We want your name.
Yes, we must have that.
No name? Paste the stamps
from your forehead onto the page.

We take what we can.
Numbers, we want them all.
This might hurt a bit.
When the tears come,
seal them in the tiny envelopes provided.

We will accept cotton pockets
in place of envelopes.
Your hands must be in them.

Stare at the third page till you see
yourself. Tear out your eyes
along the perforation.
Keep them for your records.

The buzzing you hear is normal.
The bells are not. Let the doctor push
his ring-finger between your ribs
to stop the swinging. Move carefully

for four months. Swallow
no ice. If you need to cough
use sign language, unless
you have sent us your hands.
In that case, we cannot help you.

Hub 2000

I looked at my work schedule for the last time.

As my downcast eyes looked away, I crumpled the paper in my hand and rested my cheek against the window. The bus had been driving through serpentine two-lane swaths of airport runway for the last thirty minutes. In the distance, I heard the spooling up and thrust reduction sounds of airplanes growing louder as we approached the warehouse.

The bus veered to the left and began slowing. I bent my knees slightly to absorb the motion. When the bus stopped at the last pickup point, I looked straight ahead, silently counting down the seconds. This would be my last five minute midnight stop at the Hub2000 employee terminal. After four years of working the graveyard shift for United Parcel Service, I would be moving away from Louisville with a business degree and the hopes of a career.

Several employees filed out of the last terminal, an elongated building with soaring glass walls and a flowing roof line. The driver lurched forward and pulled back on the lever, opening the doors. Most of the men quietly got on and plopped down in a seat close to the front of the bus. They're smart: the closer you are to the front of the bus, the smoother the ride to the warehouse will be. But I liked the anonymity and silence that came from sitting in the rear of the vehicle.

The bus doors nearly closed when someone close to the driver yelped. The driver bounced upright slightly in his chair and sighed. He swung the lever again, reopening the doors as another worker stumbled up the steps.

Once he collected himself, the lithe figure at the front of the bus leaned into the driver and began speaking. The driver dismissed him with the wave of a hand and released the parking brake.

His shadow came into focus as he scoured the bus. Some men leaned against the window, others talked quietly to one another, but nobody seemed interested in relinquishing any seat space. The bus began moving forward and he grabbed the back of an empty seat. By standing diagonally in the bus, he achieved the lateral stability he needed to walk forward. Still, standing up on this bus was like trying to stay on your feet on a skateboard.

He locked eyes with me and did not relinquish the stare. He grinned and kept approaching. I closed my eyes for a moment and when I re-opened them, he sat down in the seat in front of me.

Before I could take a deep breath, he turned sideways. "I'm Bryce Byrnes. This is my first day."

I blinked. "I'm Owen. Owen Halloway. You have all of the rookie excitement. I remember those days."

The corners of his mouth drew up into a smile. "This job is going to be great. I can get my tuition paid for at Jefferson CTC and still take classes during the day. I'm stoked!"

I felt the same way when I signed on to work for UPS at the Worldport. Its Owenname is the Hub2000, after UPS spent millions of dollars in 2000 at Louisville International Airport building new warehouses and constructing new runways for their planes. Many of the jobs at the Hub2000 are part-time and overnight, which are attractive prospects for college students.

When I fretted about how I was going to able to go to school and find a job that would help pay the bills while at the University of Louisville, a financial aid counselor recommended talking to a recruiter with UPS. I made my way to the career fair and immediately met with the recruiter. At first, I was intimidated by the burly man with short-cropped hair and dark eyes that seemed fixed in an intense expression. He told me that UPS offers tuition reimbursement program where students who work part time overnight can receive 100% tuition reimbursement, plus earn $10.00 an hour wage. When I accepted the job, I was surprised to learn on my first day that most of the student workers at the Hub2000 are students.

Bryce rubbed both hands together. He was an elegant boy with high-planed cheeks, wide-eyes and light curly brown hair.

"Did you know that the Hub is the size of 80 football fields and is capable of handling 84 packages a second, or 416,000 per hour?"

I cocked my head sideways and let it nudge the glass window again. "No, I didn't, but thanks for that information."

Bryce laid his palms flat and pushed himself up from the seat until he rested on his knees. He leaned over the seat.

"What's your name? I hope we can work together."

"I'm Owen," I said, feigning a smile. "We probably won't be working together because this is my last night working at the Hub."

Bryce chewed on the inside of his cheek, letting the statement resonate for a moment. "Then maybe you can introduce me to some people. I'm from Hodgenville and I don't know anybody in Louisville. Shoot, I've never done anything that paid ten dollars an hour!"

Before I could respond, Bryce cut me off. "What's it like working here? It's it fun? Do we stay busy? Is your boss nice?" His animated face dimmed a bit as a shadow washed over the bus when we passed through the runway lights and the terminal lights from the south passenger terminal of the airport.

The bus jerked to a stop and I nodded at Bryce. "You'll learn more tonight." I leaned away from the window, a bit surprised that my shoulders had gone to sleep. I rolled them, trying to get that sensation of needles floating in my skin to go away.

Bryce got up and looked down, running his hands over his uniform, smoothing out the wrinkles. He was wearing the standard issued chocolate brown attire; the button down shirt hugging him tightly. However, he was wearing shorts, although he got the socks

89

right. We are allowed to wear shorts instead of pants, but we have to purchase UPS approved brown socks.

I let out a soft laugh as we moved to the front of the bus. "Your knees are going to get skinned up wearing shorts. The steel floors of those Boeing 757's are pretty unforgiving."

He turned back to me for a moment and furrowed his brow. "We will be working on our hands and knees?"

I nodded again. "Yep. A lot."

Once off the bus, I step past Bryce and began walking to the warehouse, although I hear him taking long strides behind me, trying to catch up. A few hundred yards away from the warehouse, I see a UPS 757 shooting down a runway, although the plane emanates a loud, growling noise. I've learned that the growl means the pilots are not performing a full thrust takeoff, which usually means the plane is not full of cargo.

The one-story, brown-brick warehouse has three corrugated metal airplane hangar doors that are open. Another door near the end of the warehouse is made of thick steel and is closed. There are no windows in front, and not a single sign to identify who or what might be inside.

As the group approaches the doors, the silhouette of a Boeing 757 becomes more defined as the overhead lights bathe the inside hangar in a soft, white light. The light accentuates the two turbofan engines, tail, and supercritical wing designs which give the wings a flattened upper surface. The plane appears stately in its stoic condition, although the rear hatch doors are open and the platform ramp has already been nestled against the butt of the plane.

I turn away from the aircraft and head to the time clock room to punch in and begin my shift. Before I get close, Bryce grabs my arm.

I groan and he walks around me. "Is this it? Is this our hanger?" He steps back and cranes his neck up, examining the plane with wide-eyed optimism. "Amazing! What do we do? I know. I bet we need to climb up the ramp and start unloading."

Bryce runs to the ramp. I grab the arm of a colleague passing by, whose bright blue eyes fix on me with a wistful expression.

"Go get Mike. Tell him we have a rookie."

He walks faster towards the time clock room, hollering Mike's name. I run behind Bryce, who is now standing half-way up the platform ramp.

"What are you doing?" I ask in frustration.

He ignores me. I watch as he touches his index finger to his forehead in spontaneous meditation. "I bet we move the heavy packages out first. They are the heaviest and will take the most time to move." He snaps his fingers. "Right."

"Stop! Get your ass down from there!"

I feel Mike's warm breath on my neck through his heavy pants and heaves. Bryce freezes, then slowly backpedals down the ramp and turns around.

Mike walks around me. He is a big, easy fellow with a trim goatee and a slight, southern drawl. But he is nobody's fool, especially for an overzealous rookie employee that he's never met.

Bryce extends both arms outward and Mike stops. "I'm sorry. I didn't mean to upset you. I'm Bryce. I'm new and I'm ready to go."

I could see Mike's shoulders bounce and see him shift his weight. "We have procedures and policies around here son. They exist for a reason. Everyone knows them and everyone follows them." He looks past Bryce and points to the inside of the plane. "If you would've injured yourself up there without the proper forms being filled out, OSHA would shut us down in a minute." The veins in Mike's neck bulged and his cheeks filled with blood. He looked Bryce over. "Besides, you might be too frail for this job anyway." Some of the other guys gathering around us sOwcnered and laughed. I patted my stomach and considered this the one time I was thankful for my husky build.

Bruce rested his hands on his narrow hips. He stuck out his chest. "I just wanted to help that's all. I know that trying to move 416,000 packages an hour means there's no time to waste…"

"Cut the bullshit, will ya?" Mike interjected. He dropped his chin and shook his head. "I know the corporate company crap they put in the brochures about this place."

"I, I just…" Bryce's stammering made some of the guys laugh harder.

"You need to know a few things son. First, we do preload. You know what that is?" Bryce arched an eyebrow, but remained silent. "In preload, all the packages from the plane are mapped based on the route schedule, keeping in mind priority deliveries and bulk items. Then, we do a morning stretch for fifteen minutes. I don't want any of my workers injuring themselves unloading packages from this plane. Then, we have a meeting to discuss general business, safety, and any new regulations. Then, and only then, do we begin unloading packages."

Mike cut a sharp look at me and lowered his voice to a low rumble. "Is he a friend of yours, Halloway?"

I shook my head. "No, sir. I just met him earlier tonight on the bus."

"Good," Mike replied. He reached a meaty hand behind me and slapped my back. "You are going to be his mentor. Show him the ropes."

"But Mike, it's my last night…"

"Doesn't matter," he said, shielding the light over his eyes with one hand and squinting. "You're one of my best workers. He can learn a lot from you tonight. Besides, it looks like we've got a light plane to unload anyway."

From the corner of my eye, I saw Bryce looking down at the stained concrete floor, tapping his foot in a nonsensical pattern and whistling quietly.

"Byrnes!" Mike said, in a voice that was smaller, but more tense.

Bryce froze and slowly met Mike's gaze. "Procedures." Mike hesitated before speaking again. "We have procedures which I am going to explain to you, but only once. Then I expect you to follow them."

Bryce bobbled his head in agreement. Mike looked at me again, this time a bit longer than before. "Watch him carefully," he said with his voice a near whisper.

"I will," I replied.

Mike motioned for Bryce to follow him and immediately the crew and I assumed our usual work stations throughout the hangar.

Most of my co-workers ran to the left quadrant of the hangar and turned on the conveyor belts. In a few minutes, the belts would rise and fall as packages of all sizes whizzed by in multiple directions.

I climbed the ramp with George, a compact sophomore at the University of Louisville who had shaggy black hair, squared glasses, and arched eyebrows. The pungent smell of jet fuel still wafted through the plane, making my eyes water. The two underfloor cargo holds of the plane seemed deep and cavernous, although the open lower deck doors, when closed, divided the smaller space in the forward compartment from the deeper space in the aft one. We began pulling the packages off and sliding them down the ramp.

A few guys at the bottom collected them, and walked them over to the first conveyor belt. For a while, it will travel from one belt to another, and eventually will be loaded onto another dock. Then, the package will be taken from the dock and put on a truck that will take it to its final destination.

A lanky shadow approached. I saw George look up, then away.

"I don't think I've signed my name so many times in my life," Bryce said. "Mike didn't have to be such a grouch, either."

I kept unloading the packages, now fully comfortable in the hypnotic rhythm of sliding packages behind me. I hoped that Bryce would be quiet and just observe what we were doing.

93

He grabbed a small box from George and lifted it up, swiveling it in his hands and inspecting it. I peered at him, making sure he wasn't going to drop the package. George silently reached around him and pulled another package toward the ramp.

A look of concern crossed Bryce's face. He lowered the box and held it tightly against his body.

"What happens if we make a mistake?" Bryce asked.

George cleared his throat and glared at me over the tops of his glasses. "You want me to take this one or do you want it?"

The muscles in my throat tightened. I just wanted to get through the night quietly. Bryce pursed his lips, waiting for an answer.

"When we take a package from the plane, the first conveyor belt takes it with the label facing up and to the left. We have five scanners that scan the label and then use the information from the label to direct the package onto the next belt, which will get it closer to the right dock."

I leaned back against the wall of the plane, the cool steel comforting to my sweat-splotched back. Bryce nodded slowly, tightened the muscles in his face, and stared down at the package he was holding.

"But, Owen, the packages move from belt to belt without stopping."

"True. That's the beauty of the system. That's how we are able to move 416,000 packages a night."

I grinned sheepishly at Bryce and went back to work.

"Let me have that one," George commanded, reaching out and taking the box from Bryce." In one smooth motion, George snatched the box and slid it down the ramp.

"Go ahead and start grabbing the boxes and sliding them to me and George," I told Bryce. He crouched down and hesitated. "It doesn't matter what size or shape you pull first. Just get them off of the plane."

94

We pulled packages and shoved them down the ramp for a while. Mike walked past our operation several times, folding his arms and observing our work. When he passed by a second time, Bryce stopped moving.

"This one is leaking," he said, his voice slightly tinged with panic.

George and I passed each other a glance and kept working.

"Guys, I'm serious," Bryce pleaded, dropping the package between us. The box listed to one side, then fell back on its four corners.

I slid back against the curved metal of the cargo hold, not wanting to touch the box. A thick, black liquid oozed from the corner of the box and pooled on the floor.

George crept close to the liquid and sniffed. Bryce gasped. "It doesn't smell like anything," he said. "I'll get Mike."

After a few moments of confusion, Mike removing the package wearing protective gloves and a mask. The liquid was slick and trickled through his fingers. A scan of the label indicated the package was from Milton Freeman, and addressed to Dustin Pike with a final destination of Saginaw, Michigan. Inside the package was supposed to be a remote controlled airplane.

"I'm going to call the airport police and fire rescue just to make sure this is nothing serious," Mike said. "In the meantime, you need to take this package outside and away from the building."

I was standing outside of a group of guys that encircled Mike and I did not observe who was involved with the directive. The whispered asides of the other guys caught my attention.

"Halloway, you and Byrnes take this thing about back and sit it in that open space between the hangars."

I looked at Mike and his thoughtful, hooded eyes. Bryce looked at me, with his customary facial expression of a faintly smiling, middle distance squint of someone lost in abstraction.

"Now!," Mike barked. "We've got work to do and deadlines to meet."

I groaned, slouched my shoulders and strode towards Mike, taking the package from his hands without making eye contact. I walked past Bryce with nothing more than a gust or air passing between us. "Come on."

Bryce stood still. "Don't we need gloves?"

"Come on," I repeated, angrily.

We walked out the hangar doors. Turning around the building, the exterior was smudged with mildew and the once pristine brown brick had yellowed with age. The waning reflection of the moon provided some small streaks of light behind the building. As we kept walking, Dark-grey clouds loomed over the moon ominously and the small tufts of ruined grass surrounding the back of the hanger was perished and brought to despair and darkness once again.

A gravel path led away from the hanger. As we approached the wide open space between the two hangars, Bryce followed the path. I could hear the crunch of gravel under his work boots.

"Owen, did you see this? This is a restricted area out here at the end of the airport."

In fact, I had seen the square fenced area before. I never worried about it much.

Bryce charged ahead and squeezed through an opening in the rusted fence. He fiddled with a dilapidated iron latch.

"I wonder what's inside here. I can't believe UPS would put something like this here." As I came closer, I saw flecks of rust scattered on Bryce's fingertips. He rubbed them together and they fell away.

He looked back at me, his eyes glistening. "The lock on the fence is rusted loose."

"Bryce, don't...."

"Shhh," Bryce insisted. "Listen."

I let a moment pass between us. "We need to get back inside."

Bryce brushed away my gesture and then I heard it. A faint whisper that suddenly grew louder.

96

"Let me out. Let me out!"

Bryce looked back at me. "See. I told you I heard something!"

"Let me out." The voice sounded infantile at first, but then became stronger and more resounding. "Please let me out!"

"Let me out. I've been in here for so long. Please, let me out."

Bryce reached forward and stuck his hand in between the dark slat of space between the door and the metal box.

"What are you doing?"

"Letting this person out, Owen. We can't just go back inside if someone has been locked in here. That's cruel."

I swallowed hard. "Bryce don't…"

He slipped his hand inside and then yelped. "Something bit me." He jerked his hand back and blood trickled between his fingers. Bryce shook his hand in a semi-circular motion and speckles of blood landed on my uniform.

The metal door swung back and something bolted from the darkness and ran around the box. "There I go. That way."

Bryce stood up and began dappling his bleeding fingers on his pants. "What was that? Did you see it?"

I looked around. "No, just a dark flash and then I heard the pattering of feet. It went around the back of the fence."

"We need to find out what it is," Bryce said. "I'll go around one side and you go around the other."

I stepped back into the darkness. "No way. We need to get back inside and report this and get your hand bandaged."

"Not a chance," Bryce replied. "That person, or thing, attacked me and I want to see it."

Bryce quietly slithered like a snake around the left side of the fence. I groaned and went to the right. After a brief pause, the voice spoke again.

"It's going that way. That way."

I ran back around the fence, and I tripped over the leaking paint package and fell in front of Bryce.

"There I go. That way."

We scrambled to our feet. Suddenly, a motion light from the rear of the warehouse bathed our location in a soft hue of white light.

Standing in front of us was a jackrabbit, with antelope horns and a pheasant's tail. It reared back and sat on his haunches. Its thin lips quivered and it spoke again.

"I'm going that way. Thanks for letting me out."

The rabbit leaped over Bryce and latched onto my shirt. The sharp horns burrowed through the fabric, tearing it while the tips of the horns jabbed into my flesh. Blood began oozing from the puncture wounds and I screamed.

Instinctively, I grabbed the rabbit and flung him into the field beside the fence. I heard a thud, then the rustling of feet again. The sound appeared to surround us.

"There I go. That way."

Bryce stood motionless. "What do we do now?" I heard nothing but the silence and occasional roar of planes taking off.

Something whisked by my ear and ricocheted against the fence. Before I had time to look, another small object hit it, then another. I smelled Sulfur.

"What in the world was that?" Bryce stood up and I shoved him down. Two more small objects missed us and hit the fence. Near Bryce's foot, I saw a shell casing.

"Come on, move!"

Bryce and I crawled around to the back side of the fence. For a moment, the shooting stopped. My heart banged against the wall of my chest and my throat felt dry and hoarse. Bryce looked at me with clenched fists.

"There I go. That way."

I stuck my head around both sides of the fence. The motion light had shut off. The darkness was so thick that the area behind the field merged with the sky. I couldn't see any protruding objects, like a gun barrel, in the darkness. I crawled around to the left side of the fence, locking my fingers inside the metal holes to keep my balance.

I rose up for a moment. Another bullet zipped by me. A small wisp of smoke curled up from the cloth as I dropped to the ground again.

"There I go. That way."

The pounding in my chest now resonated in my head. Behind me, Bryce slid to the opposite side of square restricted area and I called out. "We are employees of UPS. Please don't shoot."

"Shut up! You don't know who you are talking too."

Bryce looked sideways at the fence and then straight ahead. "I don't think the details are too important right now."

Ahead, I heard some movements. "Did you hear that?"

"No," he whispered.

I heard the muffled rustling again. Another shot was fired. This time, the bullet clipped the top of the fence in front of Bryce. He collapsed flat on the ground tucked his hands behind his head.

"Man, I'm getting scared now."

"Quiet."

The movement stopped. I held my breath. Bryce remained motionless. The luminous moon glowed in the sky above. The rustling movements of what I presumed was the rabbit began to slow down and then they stopped.

"Bryce?"

"Yeah?"

"How fast can you run?"

I heard him swallow hard and cluck his tongue. "Pretty fast I guess."

"Good. I have a plan. I am going run in the direction of the shots and act as a diversion. I want you to run as fast as you can to the hangar and get help. Then come back. Got it?"

Bryce blinked at me twice, and he seemed to be grasping for the point of an anecdote that fluttered out of reach. "What if that horned rabbit attacks you again?"

Staring sternly into the pitch black darkness, I found my eyes cautiously staring at every detail in sight. "I'm not sure if it'll work, but I am out of ideas unless you have any?"

"Alright. One, two, THREE!"

I charged ahead into the darkness with my hands open, trying to feel anything in front of me. Something grabbed my wrists and pulled me further into what seemed like a dark abyss.

From behind, I heard a bump and thud.

A pause ensued, followed by a shriek. I heard a grotesque squelching noise as Bryce screamed, "Get away from me!"

I grabbed at the large hands holding my and shook one arm free. Before I could plant my feet, a punch came hurdling at my face. I was thrown to the ground. From the corner of my eye, I saw the motion light on the rear of the building come back on. Another curdling scream echoed into the night.

The shadow standing over me was burly and slightly hunched. As it reached down to punch me again, I leaned up and rammed my head into it. The shadowed stumbled backwards. I grabbed an arm and twisted it with all of my strength. The cracking of bones punctured the air.

I scrambled to my feet. Bryce bounced to me, gooey streams of blood running out of his nose.

He swiped the blood with the back of his wrist. "That rabbit tried chewing my nose."

"Are you going to be okay?" I asked him.

"Yeah." His face crinkled at the edges as he got closer to me.

My skin felt hot and I could feel pockets of flesh pulling together and protruding out from my face. "What in the hell is that thing? That rabbit?"

A trim man, with a mustache so neat that it seemed penciled in was lying on his back with one eye swollen shut and large gash on his face. He wore camouflaged pants and an orange vest. We walked over to the person. The man wallowed on the ground and moaned.

100

I grabbed him by the collar. His eyes flung open instantly and his face was all gathered up in worry.

"Let me go, please."

The man's voice was disarming. I tugged more aggressively on the collar. "I don't think so. You tried to shoot me and my friend."

"I'm sorry," he said, the shimmering beginnings of tears welled up in his eyes. "I was here hunting the Jackalope."

I shot Bryce a disbelieving glance. "Jackalope? What are you talking about?"

He leveled a stare at me. "The Jackalope…a rabbit with horns. The females produce a milk that can cure all types of diseases. Jed and I heard rumors about one of them getting on one of these planes by mistake. We've been sitting out here at night for a few weeks. We think we've seen some of them darting back and forth towards that fence." He paused and nodded in the direction of the fence. "Recently, it sounded like one had been trapped inside that metal box inside that fence. We hoped to kill it, milk it, stuff it, and the sell the milk for money."

I cut him off. "Do we look like rabbits to you? Why did you shoot at us?"

The man stammered. "I'm sorry…it was dark, we couldn't see. The jackalope is fast and if you don't take a shot when you think you have it, you'll never catch it."

I began shivering from anger and adrenaline. "That, that Jackalope attacked Bryce and I." "They can be quite aggressive if they feel provoked or threatened," the man said.

"But we called out to you," Bryce interjected. "We told you we were UPS employees and what we were doing."

"Aw," the man replied, in fussy tone that reminded me of a child preparing to throw a tantrum. "With those planes taking off all the time, it's hard to hear sometimes."

The voice returned, silencing us. "Thank you for letting me out. Now here we come."

"Stay still," the man commanded. "Let me get my flashlight." He turned into the darkness behind him and produced a flashlight.

The man shined the light around us. Surrounding us were hundreds of Jackalopes, with their horns jutting from their skulls.

"There we go….that way!"

"Owen…." Bryce said, his voice trailing away.

I closed my eyes and waited as the Jackalopes leaped onto us and began stabbing and gnawing on our flesh.

As I struggled to dislodge them from my skin, pain surged through my body and blood trickled from my arms. The blood began to pool on the ground in front of me. I heard a muffled scream as the swarm of jackalopes toppled Bryce to the ground.

"Help me!" Bryce bellowed.

The weight of the jackalopes began to drag me to the ground. The pain of their teeth pulling at my skin was unbearable.

"Here we come. There we go. We are going to put you in the box". As I rolled over on my side to reach out for Bryce, the jackalopes scurried ahead, carrying Bryce and the moaning man toward the box with their teeth.

"There we go. There you go. Back in the box."

I began to lose consciousness as the screams of Bryce and the man echoed into the night.

I Am Still Waiting for This to Pass

Beware the girl who loves *Paradise Lost,* that myth not yet
broken with the dawn. She claims Temptation while dressed
in snakeskin sandals. Delight in judging the curious as we blanket
ourselves in theories, luck, superstition's cold kiss. Find comfort
from each bad event, sparse paychecks, fragmented friendships,
a father's fists. Think to yourself *It has to be time for a break* even
as we ceaselessly break ourselves on the backs of gods, this balance
theory slipped from a myriad religions' quilts, stolen stitches fashion
haphazard agnosticism. When madness takes root, what to worship?
Spurn each old lesson, your too-tight fist trailing sand. Instead demand
Coyote, Reason, leprechauns, Mayan calendars, Yggdrasil, pharaohs
trapped in tombs erected in painstakingly precise angles.

One day, a young man makes a girl in his own image because he is
afraid. Alone in the forest, no one hears when they fall.

For Neither Can We Carry

They pulled a body out of the river when I was nine. The water had begun to freeze and they had to chip the ice away. My father read about it in the newspaper the next day. Gary Bailsey jumped off the bridge when he found his wife with another man. That part wasn't in the paper. Our town was small then. His wife disappeared not long after the funeral. I knew these things and could only appreciate the weight of them, fragments of the adult world, with the small deference of a child. I never saw the body, but there were pictures of police and firemen on the banks of the river in the paper. I still think about it whenever I'm near water. Thirty years later, I still think about it.

* * *

High up on the church, garland and a star adorn the steeple, silver and gold ring steel against the sky. The church sits at the end of a square in the town I grew up in. My parents still live here. The town is bigger then it was when I lived here. I walk into a coffee shop and order a tea. I sit by the window. A group of kids come in. College students home for break.

"Jake's picking us up at twelve," a girl says.

"I have to go home first," says another.

"Make sure to keep away from his older brother," a boy says.

"Why?"

"He's a pervert."

They leave. I watch them walk down the street. I look at the girls' asses. Firm. Young. A lady wearing too much makeup, probably my age, I can't tell, looks at me from the condiment bar. I feel her eyes. I feel like Jake's brother.

The door opens and a woman goes to the counter and orders a coffee. She pays and looks over.

"Dean?" she says.

She takes her drink and comes to my table.

"Dean Baker?"

"Maggie?"

We went to school together and had the same friends. She gives me her number to meet for drinks. She has to get back to work.

"Tonight?" she says.

"Ok," I say.

"I'm glad I ran into you," she says. She lingers.

"Me too," I offer back.

"See you tonight," she says.

* * *

I walk around town past the old shops and new shops. On Main Street, restaurants and bars filled the once vacant storefronts. The tiled entries from their former lives sit, lapidary, ignored. The druggist, jeweler, baker—people dead and gone, people no longer needed. There's a canal that runs behind the street. It's old and was built when industry was powered by water. I can see the ducks huddled on a small landmass. I am getting cold and think of my wife. We fed the ducks the last time we were here. She told me a duck's quack doesn't echo. That it is a naturally decaying sound. I turn away from the canal. Some things happen once and are never repeated. Can't be undone. I go to my car and drive to my parents' house.

We sit in the sunroom around an old wood-burning stove. It keeps us warm and heats the house. In the cold months we lay corn bags on the flat top of the stove. I take one and put it in my lap and turn it with my hands.

"Is it warm enough?" my mother asks.

"Warm enough," I say.

"It's going to be a cold winter," my father says.

"Colder than last year, they say," my mother says.

105

* * *

It snowed during Laura's funeral. It was the start of a blizzard. We stood around the grave. The ground was frozen and laid in solid pieces. The priest said words and my father and my mother were there. I have this vision of a painting—black forms clustered, grey streaks. I think of Rembrandt and darkness. Laura and I didn't have any children. We were waiting. I remember thinking I wished we hadn't. I still wish that. I remember the cold and I think of our children. I know they don't exist. I think she is somewhere with them.

* * *

"Dean," my mother says, "Are you ok?"

"Yes," I say, "Just daydreaming."

My parents share a look.

"I'm fine," I say.

I go outside to load up firewood for the night. I put on the leather apron and lift up the skirt and lay wood across. This is a different life. My parents won't be able to do it much longer. They're ok for now, not too old. Had me when they left high school. Right before my father went to Vietnam. There's a picture in the dining room of him in uniform, holding me—back when he had his own ambitions and life ahead of him. I'm older now than he was in the picture and in all of my childhood memories. I'm in the middle. I went to a doctor for a while and told him these things. He said I was experiencing "separation." "No shit," I said back. I apologized—it wasn't his fault. "I've heard worse," he said. "It gets better," he said later. I hadn't heard a doctor say that in a long time.

* * *

Inside I load wood into the stove and put the extra logs in a basket. I go to the kitchen.

"That should be enough for tonight," I say. I wash my hands in the sink and put on my jacket.

"Heading out?" my father asks.

"Yeah. Ran into an old friend."

106

"Be careful," my mother says. "It's supposed to start snowing later tonight."

"Ok."

* * *

I drive into town and circle around for a while before parking. I feel like I'm someone else. Like I'm watching this happen. I walk to the bar. I think of Laura. It seems long ago—it seems yesterday, this morning. The last months she was in the hospital, stable, then it was quick. I prepared for her death every day—she would recover a little, and then slip further.

I can see Maggie through the window. I think about leaving. She looks out and sees me and smiles. I wave to her and go inside and sit down.

"Hi," she says.

"Hi. Sorry I'm late."

"It's ok. Take your jacket off, stay a while." She laughs.

She is wearing a purple sweater. Black skirt. She looks good. Her perfume is clean. I've smelled it before. Her eyes are clear and soft in the twilight of the bar.

I order a gin and tonic. Lemon.

She orders one too.

"How have you been," she says.

"Occupied," I say.

We talk about our jobs. We talk about high school. We talk about nothing. She excuses herself and I follow her with my eyes. Her body moves under her clothes. When she comes back she is different, like someone suspended on the upside of a seesaw. She picks at her napkin.

"I'm sorry about your wife," she says.

"Thank you," I say.

"Poor thing," she says, "I can't imagine."

"It's ok."

It's not.

I order another drink.

107

Her hand is on my leg.

It feels heavy. I want it there. I don't want it there. I put my hand on the small of her back as we leave the bar, and feel her movement.

We are back at her apartment. She is divorced. Kids at their father's. She puts music on and keeps the lights low. Her breasts push against her sweater as she pulls it over her head. Her body is familiar. Her fingers are on me. Grabbing. She lowers herself, wrapping me in warm velvet.

* * *

She is asleep next to me. It is quiet and she is beautiful.

I get dressed and leave.

It's snowing outside and the street lights are surrounded by muted halos. I walk to my car and get in. The engine chokes and won't turn over. Needs a new battery. Meant to do that before I drove out to my parents. I've forgotten to do a lot of things lately. I'll have to walk home. I think of Maggie, home, asleep, warm in bed. I could go back, make up an excuse if she wakes up. I head toward my parents' house. It never happened. It never happened.

It's not that cold once I get moving. I walk through town and I'm the last man in the world. The long stretch of Main Street, its store lights and front windows dim, lay under a coat of snow. More comes down. My feet crunch and I feel bad. I turn back and see my footprints on the sidewalk and think of a picture my mother has in the kitchen of two sets of footprints in the sand. Then there is one. That's when God carries. I look at my footprints, vanishing, filling in with snow. I feel alone.

I have to cross the bridge. I'm not sure which side Gary jumped from. The river flows to the east, yes, that's the side he would have gone over. Halfway across the bridge I stop. I can see the high reaches of the church lit up back in town. I look over the railing at the river. It isn't moving. It's frozen and covered in snow. I could walk across it. He must have been here just before the freeze. I step up on to the

108

lowest rail of the bridge. And then the next. It doesn't look that high, but water is hard. Goddamnit Gary.

I climb back down and go home. I throw some wood in the stove and go to my room. I don't bother getting undressed. Sleep doesn't come. I think of last Christmas, our last one. I held her hand and she smiled at me. I remember the feel of her hand. I can't see her face in my mind. It's getting away from me.

We brought nothing into this world, the priest said. He said a lot of things. I didn't know him and didn't fault him for that. Everybody's got a job. Snow fell to the bottom of Laura's grave and clung to the walls – ridges and ledges etched in white. Not far off, behind a mausoleum, two men stood smoking cigarettes, leaning against a backhoe. They had a job too, and someday they would die and somebody they didn't know would say things and put dirt on their grave.

* * *

A knock on my door.

"Dean?" my father says.

I wake up, a sharp inhale, a yawn.

"You in there?" he says.

"Yeah."

The door opens. He comes in and sits down next to me on the bed.

"Where's your car?"

"The battery died."

"We'll take care of that today."

"Ok."

He pats my leg.

"Your mother kept a plate warm for you."

"Ok."

He gets up and walks to the door.

"Dean," he says, his hand on the doorknob.

I raise my eyebrows.

"Take your time," he says.

109

I get a shower and the water feels good. I wash myself, then turn up the hot water and stand there and let the steam surround me.

After breakfast we drive into town. The snow stopped sometime this morning. Two inches, but the roads are slow. My father gives me a jump and I drive my car to the garage. My father suggests a movie.

"I've been going to the movies a lot," he says.

"How come?"

"I thought retirement would be different, I suppose."

"Different how?"

"I don't know," he says. "Not like this."

"What's mom think?"

"She seems ok. She wants to start a garden in the spring."

"Flowers?"

"Vegetables."

"Flowers would be nice, too."

* * *

There's a theater that plays old movies during the day. They are showing one I haven't seen. My father hadn't seen it in a long time. A detective is hired by a man to spy on his wife who he fears is being unfaithful. The detective falls in love with the woman.

The movie ends with the two of them, the woman and the detective, driving over the Mexican border, and fades out with a shot of a gun in her purse.

We walk back to the shop. My car is ready.

My father wants to go to the market to pick up some fish and potatoes for dinner. I told him I want to stay in town for a little while longer.

"Ok," he says.

"I'll be home in an hour or two," I say.

I walk down to the canal and lean against the railing. I used to go fishing here when I was a boy. I caught a catfish once and brought it home. My father showed me how to clean it and when my mother saw

110

what we were doing she wouldn't let us cook it. Said it wasn't safe. We had to throw it out.

My phone buzzes. It's a message from Maggie.

"*Sorry about last night*," it says.

I'm not sure what to write back and put my phone away.

I think of the movie. I think of Laura. We always said we wanted to watch the old movies together.

I walk back towards my car and I can see the church above the small buildings. It's grey and looks wet where there isn't snow. There are men on ladders, on the roof, taking down the decorations. They are chipping away at ice surrounding the drains. It comes off in small measures and falls away, down, past stained glass windows and statues of saints, the bigger pieces catch the sun and glint before landing on the ground, where they will melt, and eventually evaporate, carrying nothing out.

Pathos

The pigeons grubbing on the lawn in the rain
are startled by a gust blowing metal onto wood,
the sound of this house chafing itself.
The rain has been falling for three days on
the moss-covered roof. The distant sirens are
reminders that this is the season of
power outages and flood warnings. More remote
is the chance that a victim's body has been found
in an apartment. His neighbors remember his
kind smile, the small talk he made at the mailboxes.
Lying on the floor with his astonished mouth
open, he seems to be absorbed in his own joy.
But the dead don't need to smile for anyone.

Today I swatted a big housefly.
I washed its corpse down the drain and
hoped its vanishing act would take
my fascination for the tragic with it.
Afterward, in the silence, the pigeons feasting
again on worms hidden in the lawn, I thought
I heard the sound of a giant whisk scraping across
the shakes, coming to stir this house in as
the missing ingredient for some recipe of
unforeseen calamity. But it was only
the rain slapping the roof and drainpipe.
The rain pities what it spits on. The spot on
the ceiling grows larger, but there is no one in

the room with a camera to record it.
The room is too white and stainless.
The spot sits above our heads
as we anticipate the next few days
of forlorn sirens. They are coming to
find us here motionless, waiting for
complications, as we watch the pigeons
in the rain, obeying their ruthless hunger.

Music

after a painting by Remedios Varo

To make music one must assemble
the verdant green from a leaf.
Carnelian and ochre from flowers,
the weight of stones.
The invisible.
One must learn to listen for songs.
The rhythm of ocean as it takes the shore.
The sizzle of woodsong seized by flame.
Gather these like shells. Or paper clips.
Create a mosaic.
Understanding, the framework.
Silence, the unexpected grout.

Check All That Apply

Stephen Sawyer waited for Talia outside Cut Above, the organic hair salon, on a misty Friday evening. He paced the sidewalk while he waited, resisting the urge to take some folded papers out of his raincoat pocket. He knew that once he started on them he wouldn't be able to stop. Finally the salon door opened and Talia floated out amidst wafts of aromatic shampoo.

He kissed her. "Do you want to eat at A. Elephant Walk, B. Anna's, or C. Washington Square Tavern?"

"Do we have to talk in outlines?" she said, laughing. "Anna's. Is that B?"

They set off up the street. "I need to stop at Pier One to get some stuff for the apartment," she said, taking his arm.

"Like what? The apartment's crammed full of stuff."

"I mean for my apartment, downstairs. My mother'll never believe I live there."

Her mother was coming tomorrow from Amherst for the weekend. This was the first time she'd visited since Talia had moved in with him three months ago, keeping her downstairs apartment until the lease ran out in June. The three of them were having dinner at a fancy South End restaurant tomorrow night.

"You didn't tell her you moved in with me?" he said.

"Let's wait until she knows you better."

He took her hand. "I'll miss you." Her lavish black hair shone, dark and bright at the same time. She'd made up her mind and it was useless arguing. Talia never doubted or second-guessed herself. She did get a little defensive, though, as if her mother's opinion of him meant more to her than she let on.

"It's just for the weekend," she said, "then I'll come back up."

They were standing in front of a bright window filled with wicker furniture and hanging lamps. "You go in," he said. "I'll be right there." He gestured at the row of shops lining the street as if he had a dozen errands to do.

He walked away as soon as she entered the store, turning down an alley between a wine shop and a fancy paper store and emerging in front of an elegant new hotel. There was a little triangle of cobblestones and struggling weeds across from the hotel, with a pair of granite benches. He sat drumming his fingers on the edge of the hard stone. Finally, he extracted the folded papers and a pencil from his pocket, unable to resist any longer. He just needed to get through the weekend, then he would quit for good.

He blazed through an employee satisfaction survey in three parts, then a card asking him to rate and review his recent purchase of an electric shaver. He flipped the card over. Please give us your thoughts (whether large or small in scope, direct or oblique, good or bad) on any aspect of your consumer experience. That left it wide open, almost too wide.

Take a minute to tell us who you are. This was better. Sawyer loved the concrete specificity of demographic information: male, single, 20-30, lives with roommate in rental unit, income less than 40,000/year, employment... he scanned the categories, filling in the bubble next to "Management." He worked in the admissions office of the college he had attended, reviewing applications and coordinating interviews. How gratifying that someone was interested in his most arcane and trivial details. He had loved standardized tests in grade school, printing his name in block letters then coloring in the corresponding circles until he closed off the final white speck in the middle.

He unfolded a Life Satisfaction survey that promised to enlighten him about his personal goals, wishes, hopes, and dreams. These were his favorite: surveys that sought to pin down the intangible. There was

116

no right or wrong, just his own truth. He circled numbers, dithered between strongly agree and partly agree, ranked items in order of importance. Rate the amount of free choice and control he had over his life on a scale of one to seven. He gave it a six and tallied his answers, landing in the authenticity and responsibility quadrant of the survey's values matrix.

How much free choice and control did Talia have? How much did she need? She had taken control of the weekend, leaving nothing about her mother's visit to chance, from the restaurant where they were having dinner, to brunch with her mother and two girlfriends on Sunday, to the lived-in look of her erstwhile apartment. He took the survey again, pretending to be Talia. She fell in the idealism and autonomy quadrant: she was self-reliant and in control of her own destiny. He didn't need a survey to tell him she was born with her shit together.

Sawyer's heart beat faster. He felt buoyed up yet calmer. The weeds stood straighter; the grass, which had the beaten down look of early spring, was tinged with light green. The setting sun turned the gathering clouds silvery-gray. Talia stood in front of him, the buttons of her coat gleaming.

"Where were you?" she said. "I thought you were coming in."

He shoved the papers in his coat pocket and gestured to the shopping bag she was holding. "Looks like you didn't need me. Let's go eat."

Sawyer was pleased to find that Anna's valued his opinion enough to slip him a survey card with the check. He started to fill it out while they waited for the waitress to bring his change. Rate your meal on a scale of one to ten, the speed with which you were seated, the attention of our staff. Write additional comments here.

Talia sipped her lemonade. "Why bother? They don't read them. I've been coming here forever and nothing ever changes."

117

He pointed to the card. "It says here they highly value my opinion."

"Oh, Sawyer, you're so…"

He tossed the card down on the table and said breezily, "You're right, why bother?"

"Sweet. And innocent, I was going to say." She stood. "I'll be right back. Ladies' Room."

Sawyer snatched up the card and began circling high numbers. He figured the restaurant wasn't looking for criticism. Praise was the thing, positive comments and lots of tens. He never wrote anything negative. The world pleased him, largely, though from time to time he offered suggestions. He wrote "the ends of the burritos could be closed in a neater fashion, perhaps glued together with refried beans."

Outside, the streetlights had come on and the sidewalk was crowded with students and young couples heading out for the evening. "Remember those surveys in Cosmo we used to do?" Sawyer said.

"Those were good for laughs. But still a waste of time."

"What about surveys used for scientific research?"

"Then there has to be objectivity, a control group, a random sample."

"What about survey results? Aren't they useful?"

"So many of them just prove the obvious. Bacon isn't good for you. Exercise helps keep weight off." Talia was no slouch. She worked as a pediatric nurse and read the Globe every day.

Sawyer loved survey results, even when the research proved the obvious. "I heard on NPR about a survey where they asked people's opinions about God," he said, "approval ratings for creation, handling of natural disasters, things like that."

Talia laughed.

"God got high marks for creation, didn't do so well on natural disasters."

"Who would have guessed?"

118

It began to drizzle while they waited for the light at Harvard Avenue to change. A swirl of wind blew trash against his shoes. He raised his umbrella and held it over them.

"Sometimes they pay people to take surveys," he said. He'd make his living doing surveys if he could.

"There's probably not much future in it. Though it might not be much worse than what you're doing now."

Sawyer let that one go. It was no secret she wanted him to do more with his career, believed he was somehow still stuck in college because he worked there. The light changed and they crossed into their neighborhood of winding streets lined with old wooden houses. How dark the side streets seemed after the noise and bustle of Beacon Street.

Sawyer was sorry when, three blocks later, they arrived at their building, an old brick apartment house with bicycles chained to its listing porch railing. He enjoyed walking home with Talia in the rain, sharing an umbrella with their heads together. He imagined married life would be made up of little moments like this. Their talk reminded him of the amiable bickering of his parents, who were comfortable enough with each other to disagree with getting torn up about it. Their marriage was almost too good to live up to, while Talia had endured first one stepfather, who had adopted and raised her, and then another, when her mother divorced him and remarried. Now her mother had left that stepfather too. It seemed to Sawyer that it should have been the reverse, Talia with the stable family, he with a series of stepfathers.

Talia stopped downstairs to drop off her purchases and arrange her apartment for her mother's visit. She doesn't want her mother to know we live together, Sawyer thought again as he climbed the stairs to the third floor. Her mother seemed to be the only person Talia wouldn't or couldn't stand up to. He worried suddenly that he didn't know Talia as well as he thought he did.

Upstairs, he escaped into his laptop, who's fourteen by ten by one inch dimensions contained an infinite world of text polls, radio button questions with customized text, and expandable blue comment boxes.

119

He sat on the couch, feet on the coffee table, and clicked on a questionnaire entitled "Discover Yourself" that promised to launch him on a new career path both challenging and satisfying. Satisfying to Talia too, he hoped. She would be happy he was trying to find something new. What he wanted most was to make her happy.

Soon he was completely absorbed. Personal values, work-related values, functional and technical skills: the questions themselves were both challenging and satisfying. He snapped his computer shut when he heard her coming up the stairs. He picked her up and carried her into the bedroom.

"How was it, Talia?" His body tingled with pleasurable afterglow. She lay in his arms, her mass of black hair washed up across his chest. He brushed some strands from her cheek so he could see her face. "On a scale of one to ten."

"Oh, well… I don't want to get too technical here, but I'd say, maybe an eight. And a half."

"Better or worse than two nights ago?"

She rolled off him onto her stomach, clutching her pillow. "You're the one who likes to answer questions. I need to get some sleep."

Sawyer blinked. He was on the couch, Talia standing in front of him in her light blue nightgown. "What are you doing up?" she said.

What *was* he doing? The last thing he remembered was curling up around her and closing his eyes. Now he was back in the living room in his boxers, computer in his lap. He didn't even remember getting out of bed.

He tilted the screen away from her. "I was just… looking at porn." He should have thought of that sooner, had something ready to pop up onto the screen. "I'm sorry I woke you."

"I had a dream." She sat down next to him. He shut the laptop and set it next to him on the couch.

"A nightmare?"

"No, just odd. I dreamed my mother was getting married again and you and I were going to the wedding, but it was here in Boston,

120

then it wasn't her getting married, you know how dreams change all of a sudden, so…"

Sawyer took her hand and squeezed it. He lifted the top of his computer with his other hand and slid his eyes over to it. He wanted to listen to her dream and he wanted to do surveys. He wanted to do both at once.

Finally she wound down and drifted back to the bedroom with a yawn. He opened the laptop and clicked on an email from his college. "Would you like to make money in your spare time? We desperately need the honest opinions of ordinary citizens…" They needed him desperately tomorrow at four o'clock at a focus group called "Current Social Issues." They'd pay him fifty dollars. It was just the chance he'd been waiting for.

Then he remembered the dinner with her mother. He'd have to pass.

The next morning, Talia made them coffee and eggs and toast, then carried armloads of clothes downstairs, waving off his offers of help. At noon, she went to meet her mother on Newbury Street for lunch and shopping. Sawyer opened his laptop. There it was again: the focus group. It ended at seven, giving him enough time to get to the South End for dinner at eight. He left Talia a note, saying something had come up at work and he'd meet her at the restaurant.

The focus group took place in the vacant office of an old warehouse in South Boston. Sawyer took two T's to get there. He sat in a windowless room filled with men and women who looked like they'd sprouted there. Did he agree or disagree that marriage is an out-dated institution? Did marriage have to be between a man and a woman? The leader handed them each a list of traits in perspective spouses to identify on a scale of importance for "very" to "not at all." Career goals and housekeeping skills meant little to him, while mutual attraction, emotional stability and a sense of humor were very important.

At seven o'clock the leader asked if there were any volunteers who could stay for another hour or two and answer questions about child-rearing. Sawyer's mood soared. He felt giddy, as if he'd climbed a mountain. He couldn't leave now, with the highest peak in sight.

He could finish the extra stuff, and take a cab to the restaurant in time for dessert. He raised his hand.

It was after midnight when he let himself into the apartment. Talia was sitting on the couch in her blue robe, hair a dark cloud around her head, eyes wet and shining.

He sat down next to her. "I'm sorry about dinner, Talia."

"Why'd you lie to me, Stephen? Was it too much for you to come to dinner with my mother?"

That "Stephen" spelled trouble. She usually called him Sawyer. "I had to work. I'm sorry. It couldn't be helped."

She held up a hand. "Don't bother. I looked at your laptop. I know where you were. There I was at the restaurant, telling my mother you were the best thing to come my way in a long time. We order drinks and I'm still smiling and telling her about the time we went canoeing and you rescued those girls who capsized. Then we order dinner and the salad comes and my mouth is too dry to even taste it, and your phone is going straight to voicemail. I could tell she thought you were a bad choice, that I was going to follow in her footsteps. I could see the pity on her face. Pity, Stephen, and something else. I was going to be her one big success, but I'd failed her. And she was mad at me for that."

"I didn't mean for that to happen. Please forgive me."

"I don't know how," she said in a flat tone, turning away from him. "It makes me so sad when I think of how things used to be. We'd come home from work and just have fun. You were so interested in everyone and everything."

Her voice broke, and the tears she's been holding spilled over. Sawyer tried to take her in his arms, but she wouldn't let him. "It can be like that again," he said.

"How, when half the time we're together, your eyes are flashing around and you're not even with me? This whatever it is--" she waved her fingers in the air--"crazy survey thing. It's taking you away from me. Get some help."

So he liked doing surveys. Was that a crime? Words had welled up inside him while she was speaking, but when he heard her last statement, all the excuses and heartfelt apologies that might bring her back to him died in his throat.

"I don't need help," he said, his voice gone cold.

She got up and left the apartment. She wouldn't even stay and argue, a bad sign. He heard her footsteps on the stairs, then the door of her apartment two flights down banged shut, reverberating through the old building. How would he feel if he lost her? Very devastated, somewhat devastated, a little devastated, not devastated at all?

Late the next morning, Sawyer poured himself a bowl of Talia's organic flax flakes. The cereal box had a little list of multiple choice questions on it. "What's your favorite leisure time activity?" He pushed it away. He got a piece of paper from the pad Talia kept in the junk drawer. He wrote:

Check all that apply:

I am very sorry.

I know I let you down.

I want to make it up to you.

I love you.

He drew a little box next to each statement. He put a check mark in each box. He folded the paper and went downstairs and slipped it under her door.

Sawyer went downstairs when he still hadn't heard from her at two. He knocked on her door. No answer. She must still be at brunch. He tried again at three. Still no answer. Who could ignore a note like that?

Upstairs he lay down on the bed. The wind howled outside his window. Tree branches scraped the walls. He tried to think about Talia and what he would say to her when he saw her, but he couldn't focus. He couldn't even picture her face.

123

Things still might have worked out if she had come home just then, but she didn't. Another hour passed. Sawyer couldn't stop thinking about surveys, their neat columns of numbers and orderly questions, the way the whole process put him in touch with his deepest feelings and values. Finally he got up and started searching for the pile of surveys he had stashed away.

He combed through the bedroom first, then the living room, finally concluding that Talia must have thrown them out. He went through the kitchen trash, sifting through the breakfast remains, coffee grounds and eggshells, paper napkins shredded and damp with sour milk and soggy bits of flax. He left the garbage on the floor and tried the bathroom next. Groping on his knees like a heroin addict, he plunged his hands into the trash where she had crumpled his most important papers among her smelliest unspeakables. He pawed through the mess, finally finding what he wanted. He lifted the pages and peeled off a tampon, blotting blood spots from the damp paper with a wad of tissues. He sat down on the toilet seat with a survey and an enormous sense of relief.

"Do you suffer from a soft addiction?" read the title. He scanned the questions. His limbs relaxed and his breathing eased. He felt like himself for the first time that day. "Do you have a habit you resort to regularly? Do you want to change this behavior but find you can't? Has someone close to you become angry about the amount of time you devote to it?"

Surveys were everywhere. He couldn't open a newspaper or his laptop without finding one. Getting away from them was like trying to give up seeing the sky.

He was happily checking boxes when he heard the apartment door open.

"Sawyer? Are you home?"

He shaded in a box.

124

She called his name again. "I found your note after my mother left. It must have blown under the table. Do you think maybe we could talk?"

She sounded so sure of herself. He saw how it would go: I'll forgive you *if…* I'll forgive you *when*. Stealthily he turned a page.

"Okay, then," she said after a moment. "I'll be downstairs."

Sawyer raised his head. A veil lifted for an instant, a moment of awareness that everything was slipping away. Quickly he pulled it down.

Dawn Dream Merida

Buttons fasten one time to another.
Shattered fragments, a mosaic
grouted in the night.

Give me water flowing through
to float the raft of ache
and circumstance.

Ten thousand fan-tailed grackles
fracture light. Bells intone
the call to prayer.

Pipe exhaust and strident brakes
conspire with horns, muting
God's *insectos* chorus.

insectos: a Yucatecan colloquialism for the grackles

Sunday They

note written to show Lil what it seemed she was saying

Driving away from my place I noticed two
well-dressed older women on my block, one
waiting on the sidewalk while the other
approached a neighbor's house, bending
and reaching, holding something light in her hand.

When I got home later that day
I found a flyer tucked nearly invisibly
into the crack between front door and jamb.
There was an image of crucified Jesus, and I'm sorry,
church ladies, but I dumped it in the recycling.

In between I'd visited a friend rehabbing
from a brainstem stroke. She's working on swallowing,
speaking, trying to move the half of her face and body
frozen when a breakout from an overworked vessel
damaged tissue it had till then bathed with life.

By "bathed with life" I am referring to the little
bio I learned in high school, how through osmosis
waste leaves living cells and joins the bloodstream –
erythrocytes, leukocytes, and plasma pushed in pulses,
dropping off oxygen and nutrients, picking up the trash.

Sort of a food truck and garbage truck simultaneously,

127

selling tacos, samosas, or crêpes, maybe all three,
with easy-to-read bins for tossing paper, cans, bottles
here, and nasty smelly stuff there. Only, if you're a cell,
you have to have your shit lined up and be ready to order.

I know resurrection is not the same as recycling or
cellular metabolism. It's a mystery, resurrection,
one of those notions my poor little brain can't
resolve, one of those puzzles that used to
stress me out and now has just taken its place

on a shelf of curiosities, a shelf that seems to be
infinitely long, or at least unending so far, a shelf
where I keep so many wonderful things, friends
from childhood vanished beyond the reach of Facebook,
even a first wife, and grandparents so devout

their prayer books and Bibles survive on actual shelves
in my house. The health of those forebears, though,
their routines and desires, there's no shelf for all that,
no osmosis to spiff it up, no rehab like what's helping Lil.
I can imagine them smiling. That's as far as I can go.

Return

Helen's father smoked a pack of Pall Malls a day. He also believed that the Hasidic Jews who lived in Holly (two towns over) had been conspiring to buy up all the property in his neighborhood, as he'd claimed they'd done in countless others throughout central New Jersey. He'd sit at the kitchen table, smoke wafting from nostrils, and expound on his theory.

"Not that I'm an anti-Semite," he'd told Helen during one of her monthly visits. "But once one of 'em moves in, it's just a matter of time."

Helen's mother's perfunctory response: "You know your father."

He'd started a campaign to make his front lawn as unattractive as possible, which Helen found ridiculous because her parents' house was not for sale. Still, he believed that by failing to mow the lawn, weed the flowerbeds, and fix the fence post that had been snapped in half during a nasty nor'easter, no one would want to buy the Martins' place across the street that had already been on the market for three months.

"He's harmless, dear," her mother had said, waving her hand as if her husband's sabotage efforts were no more worrisome than a fly that needed shooing. "No one takes him seriously."

But after he returned home from the discount garden center with two dozen ceramic gnomes, Helen knew that some people would take him seriously. Did her mother continue to believe that her husband of forty-five years was harmless after he paired off the gnomes and placed them in sexual poses along the front walk that led down to the mailbox? To Helen, the most disturbing configuration sat under the mailbox itself: two gray-bearded gnomes 69'ing—their red pointy hats shooting out from between each other's legs.

Helen wasn't sure at what age men became harmless; her seventy-year-old father had been transformed into one of those silver-haired, arthritic men whom people simply tolerated. Once, during breakfast at Star's Diner in Allentown, her father had said to their waitress: "Tell José or Juan that the eggs were runny today." He'd never been inside the kitchen nor so much as glimpsed one of the cooks' heads peeking out from its swinging doors. The waitress had smiled and cleared their plates without saying a word. Helen wondered if she'd been too busy to correct him or if she knew that explaining why it was offensive to assume that the kitchen staff was Latino would prove futile.

And five years earlier, at Thanksgiving, her father had stood up from the table and asked Helen: "Are you a dike?"

Her mother shook her head and spooned more stuffing onto Aunt Millie's plate.

Helen refused to answer the question.

She'd never married or had children—never had a boyfriend for more than three months, either—hence her father's assumption that she was gay. Two decades before that Thanksgiving, when her father had, for the first time, inquired about her sexuality, Helen considered the idea that she might indeed be a lesbian. She wasn't sexually attracted to women, but wondered if that was because she'd never experienced a woman before. How could she know if she preferred something if she'd never tried it?

The problem: she didn't know any lesbians with whom she could experiment. When she'd finally summoned the courage to walk into a gay bar in Brooklyn, Helen discovered that none of the women cared to help her discover if she was in fact gay. No one had attempted to buy her a drink that night—so she'd bought her own. Five cranberry and vodkas later, the bartender with the crew-cut and thick black rimmed glasses told Helen that maybe she should call a cab.

Helen decided that she must be heterosexual; if she were gay, she'd thought, these women would have smelled it on her.

* * *

130

Two weeks after her father littered his front lawn with the sexually explicit gnomes, Helen lost her job. She lied and told her parents that she'd been let go from the preschool. "Cutbacks," she told them. "Seems to be happening in a lot of schools these days."

What she failed to mention: when the children were curled on spongy blue mats during nap time their shallow breathing had seemed to synchronize; with the lights off and a slight breeze coming in through the windows, Helen had joined their collective, metered breath and fallen asleep, too. By the time she woke up, the blood from Danny's severed index finger had already painted his shirt and pants, and the white tiles he stood on, a rich cerise; he hadn't shrieked or cried when the paper cutter's blade came down upon his tiny digit, and when he stood in front of the arts and crafts table—his detached finger cupped in his bloodied hand—he remained silent still.

She knew that paper cutters were forbidden—the first item, in fact, on the preschool's NOT ACCEPTABLE FOR CLASSROOM USE list. After her termination, Helen wondered where her disregard for rules came from. She often parked in loading zones, failed to yield to pedestrians at crosswalks, and refilled her beverage at the Burger King even though a sign specifically read: No Refills. As far as she could tell, poor Danny's finger had been the first casualty resulting from her need to circumvent the rules.

When her boss, Abby, pulled her into the small office that sat at the end of the school's lone hallway, Helen was unprepared for Abby's rapid-fire questions.

How often do you fall asleep under the arts and crafts table?

No, it was *not* the first time—there was a blue nap-time mat there *and* a pillow; several children have come forward and recall seeing you under there on many occasions, Helen.

Of course they didn't use that word—I know they don't know what *occasions* means.

Why did you not inform us right away after it happened?

131

No, that's not reasonable. There are five other teachers in this building who could have helped you with the other students. You know that, Helen.

At some point during Abby's interrogation, Helen reached for her throbbing ring finger—the one that always seemed to get the imbedded hangnail. The cuticle would swell and redden and contain its very own heartbeat. She usually went to extraordinary lengths to avoid touching it, but each time Abby posed another question, Helen tightened her grip and squeezed the inflamed finger. Her eyes burned. She got dizzy. And Abby's words sounded as if they'd been submerged in water, reminding Helen of her summers at the YMCA, where she'd sit at the bottom of the pool and scream as loud as she could, but no one ever heard her.

She guessed that Abby's manicured nails never suffered such afflictions. Abby never seemed to suffer, period.

You know this is bad, right?

Yes.

You know I have fire you, right?

O.K.

Abby allowed her to stay late that day to collect her things. Helen removed her favorite finger paintings from the classroom's yellow cement walls, the ones *she'd* painted alongside the children. The popsicle stick house sat on the windowsill; she couldn't bear to leave it—she'd worked too long and too hard on it.

When she arrived at her apartment that evening, she heated the end of a safety pin with a lighter. In the bathroom, over the sink, she slid the pin between nail and skin, and squeezed hard. Yellow pus seeped out and pooled on her nail.

* * *

A week later, Helen convinced her landlord to allow her out of her apartment's lease without a penalty. On the first of the month, she pulled into her parents' driveway with her Volvo packed with clothes and books and the popsicle stick house, the only items she hadn't sold on Craigslist.

"Of course you can stay here," her mother told her on the front walk, surrounded by copulating gnomes.

"Temporarily," Helen assured her mother. "Until I find another school."

Her mother dismissed this statement with a wave of her hand. Helen regarded the gnome pair next to her mother's foot: one had its face buried in the long grass; the other stood at its rear, a pipe squeezed between its lips.

On that first night back in her parents' house, after she'd hauled the black plastic garbage bags filled with clothes to the guest bedroom on the second floor, Helen collapsed on the twin mattress that butted up against the room's lone window. At some point, her mother knocked on the door—or so Helen thought; she knew she might have dreamt it. "Hungry, Helen?" she thought her mother had said.

After midnight, something moved under her pillow. Without lifting her head, Helen shot her hand underneath and searched for the culprit. She grabbed hold of some small, skinny thing. Moonlight glowed through the lace curtains, and she recognized Danny's finger, still caked in blood, fluttering in her palm. She knew it was impossible—his finger had been successfully reattached that same day he'd sliced it off—yet, she felt its warmth and, albeit slight, weight in her hand.

Downstairs, a door slammed. Helen opened her eyes, saw the pair of white Nikes still on her feet, sat up and pulled the curtains from the window. A figure stood on the front walk. After her eyes adjusted to the dark, she recognized her father as he bent down and picked up a pair of gnomes from the grass. Did her mother know he was out there?

He pulled a cigarette and matches from flannel pajama bottoms. In a single deft move, he lit the cigarette, bent down, and picked up another gnome pair from the lawn, then another. Smoke rose from his neck and shoulders. He arranged each gnome pair on the front walk, where, Helen assumed, the grass would not obstruct his presentation.

133

The only gnomes not to be relocated: the 69'ing pair under the mailbox, which sat upon gravel.

Maybe he has dementia, Helen thought.

Her father stepped on the cigarette butt while lighting a second one. After a long drag, he crossed his arms and scrutinized his gnomes.

Helen slept—for the first time in years—until eleven o'clock. After showering, she emptied the garbage bags and filled the bedroom's dresser with her clothes. Downstairs, she made coffee. A note sat on the counter. Her parents had gone to the supermarket. Did she still like Cornflakes? They would pick some up for her. And don't make plans for dinner. The Grants are coming with their son, Allen. He lost his job, too!

She vaguely remembered the Grants, her parents' neighbors and only friends for the past ten years, and hadn't been aware that they'd had a son. She knew that Mr. Grant had recently retired from teaching middle school language arts; her mother mentioned this often, along with how beloved Mr. Grant was in the community. "You should see it," her mother's familiar story began. "Everywhere he goes, former students chat him up, saying how much he'd meant to them—how much he changed their lives! Can you believe it?"

Once, Helen had thought about reminding her mother that *she* was a teacher, too—that she might have had at least *some* positive affect on her students. Mr. Grant, however, had probably never allowed a student to chop off a finger while he napped under a table. But he *must* have had his off days. Who could be expected to be at 100% all the time?

"When Allen called us and needed to return home," Mrs. Grant said at dinner, as her husband salted his pot roast, "of course we were concerned."

Helen's mother gave Allen a pat on the hand; Mrs. Grant looked upon her son, who appeared oblivious that he'd become the topic of conversation, shook her head and continued: "He's a good boy—you know that, Claire."

Her mother said, "He certainly is." She looked toward her husband. "Right, Harry?" But Helen's father stared out the window at the Martins' house across the street. A silver Lexus sat in the driveway—the realtor's car.

Helen had been told, no, *warned*, that Allen was some math or engineering wiz but had some *problems,* and that she should attempt to treat him as normal as possible. Apparently, if Allen got upset or frazzled—her mother's word—he might have one of his *episodes.* This made Helen think of Andy Russell, a former student of hers, who'd spend most of the day silently drawing or coloring. Without warning or provocation, he'd start to scream and throw whatever his hands could grab, terrifying the other children and Helen, too. The third time it happened, Helen wrapped her arms around the screaming boy, squeezed him against her chest. He fell silent. And while she wasn't sure why this assuaged Andy, she was happy to have facilitated the reprieve from the horrific pictures she imagined forever playing in his head.

Helen's gaze kept falling on Allen's curly black hair. It looked wet, but she knew it wasn't. It had had ample time to dry; before her mother served dinner, Mr. Grant had opened a bottle of red wine and discussed the impending election with her father (neither was thrilled about their choices) for what must have been thirty minutes. Allen's graying sideburns and stubble gave him away: *Dye job*, Helen thought, *and a poor one at that.*

"Of course we had room for him," Mrs. Grant said. Her husband shook his head in agreement; a wad of pot roast bulged his cheek like chewing tobacco.

Under the table, Allen removed his shoe and extended a bare foot toward Helen.

"And the Thompson's son, Frank, moved back in with them a month ago," Mrs. Grant said. "Lost his job, too—worked for one of the airlines. It's like an epidemic. Just awful."

135

Helen used her foot to push Allen's away, which seemed to send him the wrong message—he returned it with renewed determination and force. When his sweaty toes clung to her shin, then her knee, working up toward her plaid shorts, Helen attempted to make eye contact with him—to tell him with eyes what her foot had failed to say. He did not look at her, however. Once again, he seemed oblivious to his surroundings, stared at his plate and shoveled mashed potatoes into his mouth.

"Helen's sure to find *something* soon," her mother said to the Grants. "Maybe Mr. Grant can take your resumé, dear. Right, Bob? You must have connections still."

"Sure do," Mr. Grant said. "What's your certification in?"

"Certification?" Helen said, as Allen's foot lingered on her knee.

"As in what can you teach," Mr. Grant said.

Helen did not respond; instead, she reached under the table and grabbed Allen's foot; she squeezed his big toe hard enough to get his attention. Then pushed it away.

"Preschool," Helen's mother said. "Helen teaches preschool."

"I'm sure I can make a few phone calls on your behalf," Mr. Grant said. Helen's mother smiled, reached for the wine bottle, and topped off his glass.

For the first time, Allen looked at Helen. He appeared disappointed that she'd not enjoyed his foot-groping. Helen wondered where he'd been employed; that *he'd* kept a job long enough to be laid off instead of fired seemed impossible.

"That slimy realtor's sure making a killing," Helen's father said, his attention still on the Martins' place.

"Martin will be lucky to get out of there with half his money," Mr. Grant said. "Buyer's market." Both Mrs. Grant and Helen's mother pursed their lips and shook their heads.

"Just awful," Mrs. Grant said.

Helen's father scanned the table. "Wonder how he'd feel if it was *his* neighborhood. Bet you not one Jew would—"

"We've got peach cobbler," Helen's mother chirped, springing out of her chair. "I'll start the coffee. Got vanilla ice cream, too."

When her mother scurried into the kitchen, Helen took this as an opportunity to excuse herself from the table. "I'll help her with the coffee," she told them.

Her mother was busy at the sink and did not notice when Helen walked through the kitchen toward the bathroom. Only later, after the Grants left, did her mother knock on the bathroom door. Helen sat on the covered toilet seat, staring at the grout lines in the shower. "Everything all right, dear?" her mother asked.

"Fine, mom," Helen said. *Fine*, she thought, though she worried that nothing seemed fine, and that sitting in the bathroom for nearly two hours without having to so much as pee—feeling content and safe in the well-lit, confined space—was the exact opposite of *fine*.

* * *

U-Haul trucks became a familiar sight throughout the neighborhood. On weekend mornings (the busiest moving days), retractable metal ramps scraped asphalt, rousing Helen from bed. Grown children piled furniture and boxes and clothes inside their parents' garages. This downsizing reminded Helen of the big bang in reverse: universes had begun collapsing in on themselves, returning the newly unemployed children back to their origins—to the smallest speck of primordial existence. The number of cars in each driveway appeared to double, however; some children settled for parking on the street, though Helen *had* witnessed one hysterical, aproned mother, whose Lincoln sat curbside, direct her son's Mustang toward the center of the driveway like an air-traffic controller shepherding a 747 to its gate. The FoodMart on Route 35 became overrun with mothers bumping elbows and jostling for position in front of the meat and poultry section. Swollen shopping carts thronged the aisles.

One afternoon, Helen's mother came home exasperated and sweating—the deli section had run out of yellow American cheese *and* slow-roasted honey turkey breast. She'd been made to wait fifteen

137

minutes, then informed that boiled ham and swiss were her only choices—if you could believe that.

The returning children, for the most part, did not insist on special treatment or elaborate home cooked meals. In fact, they made themselves useful: lawn mowing duties were taken over for aging fathers; gutters cleaned; pools vacuumed; flowerbeds weeded.

Helen became proactive, too, and decided to take a razor blade to the rotting grout in the guest bathroom—years of soap scum and spotty mold had turned the grey lines a pus-yellow. Her father attempted to assist her, but his hands turned to stone soon after they'd started. So he sat on the covered toilet seat, chain-smoked and watched her work.

She stripped off a chunk of caulk from around the base of the tub, and asked him, "Do you think you might have gone overboard with all the gnomes?"

He sat, legs crossed, and considered her question. Then said: "Overboard with the gnomes?"

"Yes," she said. "Maybe it's time to give it a rest, you know? It's antisocial behavior, Dad—not to mention creepy."

Either he hadn't heard her or decided to change the subject. "Mr. Grant said he'll take that résumé any time you're ready."

"Right," she said, running a finger along the new space she'd created between the tiles and tub.

She'd almost lulled herself into believing that she was like the other returning children—those who could point a finger at President Bush for fucking up the last eight years, and at the too-big-to-fail banks, and the scum of the Earth who made millions off dividends and betting against bad investments. At night, however, flat on her back, staring through lace curtains, she knew that the plummeting economy had nothing to do with her termination. She was different from them. She'd caused Danny's accident. She was responsible.

"Helen," her father said, "you're bleeding."

138

She looked down, saw a fist that didn't look like hers clenching the razor blade. "Shit," she said, relaxing her hand. The nerves came alive then, sending sharp pain signals to her brain and back down to her palm, where a slender gash, lined with blood, ran parallel to her thumb.

"Here, use this," her father said, handing her a wad of toilet paper.

That night, after she'd made tea, she discovered her mother curled and asleep and snoring on the living room's sofa. She looked frail and much smaller than the woman who'd once grabbed an eight-year-old Helen by the hair and dragged her across the kitchen floor, after Helen made two proclamations: she hated her parents and would no longer accompany them to church. It now looked as if the slightest breeze would flake off her mother's skin, carry it away, and leave only brittle bones behind. She touched her mother's hand; it felt like cold tissue paper. She grabbed the blanket off the sofa's back, covered her with it.

Helen then ventured out onto the front porch, where she watched her father rearrange gnomes again. He failed to notice her as he went about his work. The late August moon provided ample illumination. Her father mumbled to himself as he squatted on the front walk. He patted the top of a gnome's long purple hat, picked it up and placed it on top of a gnome-orgy he'd been, apparently, working on for some time. He giggled and coughed and lit a cigarette.

Helen looked down the street, scanned the rows of identical houses—only their colors and variations of window treatments distinguished one from the next—and wondered how many returning children found themselves disconcerted by their parents' behavior. How many among them worried about stove burners left on for a third and fourth time? Did their parents fall asleep with lit cigarettes wedged between fingers, like her father? Did they fear, like she did, that they alone were capable of detecting the moment when the cigarette hit the floor and engulfed the shag carpet in flames? Did they worry about break-ins and floods, about carbon dioxide filling their parents' houses and killing them in their sleep? She knew that some of them must have been anxious about another harsh winter—their fathers shoveling

139

heavy, wet snow, hearts pumping too fast and hard, then giving out. Or was it just her?

* * *

She woke up at seven o'clock—downstairs, her mother made a racket with the coffee machine and frying pan. After failing to fall back asleep, she decided to join her parents for breakfast.

At the table, her father buttered rye toast; he nibbled half of it, but then put it down and turned toward the window that looked out onto the street. Her mother brought two steaming coffee mugs—said how nice it was to have all three of them eating together for once. "Your father usually stands at the counter and wolfs down breakfast like he's at the Port Authority," her mother said.

Helen reached for a cantaloupe. "Since I have you both here," she said, "it's a good time to talk about cleaning up the front yard."

Her mother hadn't sat down yet. "Speak to your father, dear," she said. "Outside's his realm."

Helen looked to her father, but his attention was fixed on the street. "So, Dad? Think it's time to retire the gnomes or what?"

Without warning he sprang to his feet, knocking over his coffee mug. Helen and her mother watched as he darted to the front door and then outside. They could see him through the windows; he ran full speed toward the mailbox, where a young couple—dressed in identical blue Nike track suits—stood, waiting for their miniature pinscher to finish peeing. The dog's skinny leg hovered above the 69'ing gnomes; piss bounced off the top gnome's red hat.

Helen's mother did not stick around to see what transpired once her husband reached the young couple: she ran into the kitchen for paper towels to clean the coffee, which had started dripping onto the wood floor. The dog was still peeing when Helen's father grabbed it and tossed its black and brown body into the middle of the street. Its head bounced off the pavement; its legs twitched. The woman— hysterical and shaking—ran into the street and scooped her dog into

140

her arms. The young man stood unmoving. Helen's father turned and headed back up the driveway.

Paper towels in hand, Helen's mother reappeared at the table just as her husband of forty-five years opened the front door. When he sat down, she said, "Watch it, Harry, floor's still wet."

Then her mother returned to the kitchen, the soaking wad of paper towels cupped in her hands.

The half-eaten piece of rye toast sat untouched; her father buttered a second one.

Outside, the young woman continued screaming.

The police said they wouldn't cuff him if he came willingly and without incident. When the police cruiser pulled out of the driveway, Helen got to work on the front lawn. She gathered all the gnomes, carried them three at a time to the garage, lined them against the back wall. Her first instinct had been smash them on the driveway—sweep them up and throw them away—but she knew her father would replace them. She decided to make a deal with him: he could keep them in the garage, pair them however he wanted to, as long as they never made it onto the lawn again. He'd fight it, she knew, but limits had to be set. *Perhaps his night in jail will make this transition easier on him*, she thought.

She checked the gas and oil levels of the lawnmower; she emptied the still-full bag of dead brown grass clippings. She walked in straight lines; stopped often to unclog the mower's blades; emptied the bag of clippings seven times. Her mother came out with iced tea. No one stopped by to thank her for cleaning up her father's mess, but she knew they must be watching from behind windows.

On her knees, she weeded the flowerbeds. She thought about how she'd only planned on staying with her parents temporarily. But the word *temporary* conjured up so many images in Helen's mind, that its definition eluded her. Was her father's insanity temporary? Maybe her job had been the temporary thing, and returning to her parents had been inevitable.

141

When he returns he'll be frightened, Helen thought, as her hands dug in the dirt. She grabbed a stubborn root and pulled.

Next door, Mr. Grant opened the trunk of his Oldsmobile, heaved a black suitcase inside.

He'll worry about losing control again.

Allen followed his mother to the passenger side door. Mr. Grant sat behind the steering wheel, adjusting the air-conditioning and checking the mirrors.

When they pulled out of the driveway, Mrs. Grant stood near the mailbox waving and smiling until the Oldsmobile rounded the corner and disappeared. She lingered curbside, shaking her head. She rubbed her palms together as if to keep them warm.

He'll slip up—need to be reminded what's acceptable behavior. But he'll try his best to be as normal as anyone else.

That autumn, U-hauls continued to fill her parents' neighborhood. Some weeks more children moved out than in; and some weeks Helen lost count.

Seconds

Dane put the tiny bit of blue-black hair inside the satin-lined box and closed it. She put it in the bedside drawer and set her iPod in the small speaker base. Music while she dressed would help.

It was over, the abstinence. She put on leggings, no underwear. The black bra teased its silhouette through a long, white shirt. A longish blazer didn't cover the shirt all the way, but both covered her butt with a hug that showed curvature. Boots went over leggings.

The Library, its logo a pile of books, was a small pub two blocks from campus and a block from her apartment. She could walk back home if she had to, escape in a hurry if this was a mistake. Checking the slot in her purse for the condoms one more time, she hit the sidewalk.

Tonight's music wasn't live performance jazz like it was on weekends. Monitors crowned the room with music videos in sync, the current song being Adele's "Rolling in the Deep."

Dane's entrance may as well have been announced with trumpets. A beautiful woman alone prompted the men to drop any pretense of shyness. Dane's stare was stuffy, disapproving, as if she were here to talk these people out of having a good time. Still, they eyed her with open hunger.

An empty seat between two men seemed a good starting place. Both men on either side gave up their companions for a go at her, speaking at once together. She wrapped her scarf around her neck and kept her eyes on the television above the bar. Even without encouragement, one man established his alpha position and backed the other man down. The second smiled as if this were a temporary situation. He was content to watch the alpha flame out.

When the bartender showed, Dane ordered dry vermouth. The bartender carded her, law in this college town no matter the age. He handed her ID back.

"Dane, is it?" the bartender said. "You don't look twenty-four."

Alpha grinned with obvious thanks to the bartender.

"Dane," the bartender said, pointing to Alpha, "meet Anderson. He's an authority on celestial bodies."

"Vermouth?" Anderson said to Dane. "Why don't you put something with it? Like gin?"

His voice was unhindered and calm in the white noise. She nodded to the bartender.

"Martini," she said.

When the bartender started to set the drink on the bar, Anderson took it before it hit the wood. He steadied the drink without spilling a drop from the shallow funnel-shaped glass. He told the bartender to put the drink on his tab and set a proprietary foot on the rungs of her stool. As she turned to look at Anderson, the power went out. Neon beer signs blinked off, and motors quit humming. The televisions were the last to give up light with dying blue screens before the room went to total darkness.

Amid exclamations and curses, Dane and Anderson remained still and quiet. Cell phones lit the room with the weak glow of small birthday candles. Their lights flashed off the ceiling and the bottles behind the bar, off drink glasses and seeing glasses, off the brass rail and lacquered tabletops.

Dane braced for a grope, but it didn't happen. She felt his hand reach across the back of her chair while his other hand still held the drink.

"A sip?" he said.

She nodded slightly. In the dim light, he brought the rim of the martini glass to her lips. She took the glass from him, expecting him to protest. He didn't. She sipped again, this one longer, holding it now

144

with both hands.

The bartender yelled the outage was temporary, the utility company was already working on it; but people began to leave anyway. Without music and television to provide anonymity, the place no longer seemed like a bar. Dane wondered if the power was off in her apartment too.

The bartender lit extra candles in small bowls. Waitresses passed out peanuts and pretzels and potato chips, informing the patrons the kitchen had to shut down. Dane could only see a vague outline of his profile, but Anderson didn't have the smell of one too long in the night's alcohol. He looked up at the ceiling.

"No stars in here," he said. "With the power off in the city, we can see the stars outside a lot better than we usually can."

Dane and Anderson moved to a small table on the pub's empty patio. Anderson was taller than she was, taller than she thought while they were sitting on the barstools.

"The bartender said you were an authority on celestial bodies," she said. "So you must be studying astronomy."

He nodded. "You're in theater? Ballet?"

"Engineering," she said.

The street was dark from the power outage, but the moon was full. It was like seeing a snowfall at night, light reflecting off any pale object. A car with a pearlized paint job, rounded at every section, glowed like a holograph in a science fiction movie.

Anderson smiled at her. "I can get you on the roof of Neison Hall. We'd have the observing telescope all to ourselves."

She didn't return the smile and leaned back into the wiry metal chair. The only small cloud in the sky dissected the moon on its way to the other side of the heavens.

"Canus Major," he said, pointing to a constellation. The longer she stared, the more stars appeared against the black night. "Monoceros. Lepus. Columbia."

"Galaxies, clusters, nebula," she said. "I'm only concerned with one place out there."

145

"Only one? Man, I wish I could live long enough to go to all those stars. So what's it with you? Gotta be the moon."

"Strange to be in a race where the finish line is taunting me."

"The finish line?" He turned to look at her. "You're on that team? The one going to the moon?"

"I wish we were going to the moon," Dane said. "We're building a lunar rover that will go in our place. It's a vehicle that can navigate the moon's surface. It has to be able to cover five hundred meters while sending back real time data."

"It's a contest, right?" he asked.

"Teams from universities all over the world are competing. How did you know about it?"

"Read about it in the student newspaper," he said. He leaned closer to her, and she caught a scent from him in the fresh air. It seemed to have less of a smell than a coolness, less of a statement than a pause. She inhaled again, looked into his eyes. The whiteness of the moon made shadows on his face, like high noon sunshine in black-and-white photos.

"What if that's a swamp up there instead of a dustbowl?" he asked.

"There's water on the moon, but not enough to make a swamp."

He kissed her, ran his lips across her cheek. "Are you so sure?"

She stood, stepped on the sidewalk outside the patio area. "I live down the block."

When she started walking, he followed. He caught up and lifted her from the ground toward the sky, the moon behind her.

She brought the back of his hand to her mouth, sneaking another smell of him like an addict sneaking a forbidden cigarette in an airplane lavatory.

"Dane," he said.

She led him to her apartment. Inside the door, he kissed her again. They melted into each other, pulling at clothes, pulling one another closer. Dane was lost. It was all movement and breathing. She distinguished fragrances and touches. Cold nutmeg, clean cotton, new

146

hay.

"Dane," he said. He took her face in his hands and looked her in the eye.

In her bedroom, the moon striped the floor with slanted light. When they were done with lovemaking, Dane watched Anderson sleep. His strong features were clearer in his shadowy profile. He was older than she thought at first, more like her own age instead of an undergrad. His lovemaking was generous and kind, something she'd hoped against—though she didn't realize it until now.

When he began snoring slightly, she crept from the bed and pulled the small box from the drawer. Opening the window a crack, she watched the black sky and breathed in cool air.

The power was still out. No lights were on in the neighboring apartments, no sounds of television or radio came through the air.

Canus Major. Monoceros. Lepus. Columbia.

It the slant of moonlight, she opened the box and unfolded the paper inside it. With her finger, she rearranged the bit of blue-black hair and began to refold the paper. The sudden touch of Anderson's hand on her shoulder made her drop the box and the paper.

"Don't move," she said.

"Are you okay?"

"I was," she said, "until you frightened me. Go away. Not here—over there. I've lost something and you'll send it scattering if you walk everywhere."

Anderson went to the bed where he put on his boxers and picked up his phone, turning it on for the light the way the bar patrons had done.

"Let me help," he said.

"No."

She hadn't moved except for her eyes covering the patch of illuminated floor. After a long moment, she saw the curl of a single black hair against the skin of her knee. She touched her middle finger to her tongue and then touched the hair to retrieve it and return it to

147

the paper. She found several more hairs on the floor and on her skin, setting each carefully on the paper. She closed the box, but she did not move.

"What time is it?" Dane asked.

"Four-sixteen a.m."

"Well, Mr. Astronomer, do you know when we'll have sunrise?"

Anderson punched a couple of icons on his phone. "Dawn is as six thirty-seven, sunrise is a seven oh-four a.m."

"Then we don't move until sunrise. Because—"

"I know. I'll just send it scattering."

He sat on the bed at first, then he lay back with his feet still on the floor. She thought he'd gone back to sleep when he spoke again.

"I'm sorry," Anderson said.

She was still naked, so she didn't have anything to wipe away the tears but her hands. He brought her a tissue and a robe from the bathroom and sat down carefully behind her, away from her search area.

"What's in the box?" he asked.

"My baby's hair. Except she's not a baby anymore. She's ten years old."

He kissed the back of her head and gently pulled her black hair away from her face, his eyes even with hers.

"Fourteen," he said. "That's young to have a baby."

They talked, the black sky turning gray so slowly they didn't notice first light. A small lamp came on before they realized the sun was up and the power was running again. Anderson got on his stomach and eyed the floor, coming in closer and closer to the site of the spill. They retrieved more individual hairs and she put them back in their place. Only when Dane signaled she was done with the search did Anderson stop looking.

Dane closed the box and clutched it with both hands.

"Cut class with me," Anderson said. "We'll hike Mt. LeConte."

Dane raised her eyes to see his face for the first time in real light.

148

He was good-looking in an efficient way, like a catalogue model. His pale eyes were tangled up in hope and anxiety.

"Can't," she said. "We had new wheels machined yesterday for the rover. It has to make a good run on the tilt table in deep sand. Just the first of many tests, and our deadline is getting too close. We can't put it off."

He stood and started to get dressed. "Will you come by the pub tonight?"

She didn't speak this time and shook her head again.

"My thirst is simple," he said. "How about I come here for a glass of water?"

"It's not a good idea."

Anderson turned off the small lamp. Sunlight replaced the moon's beam on Dane's floor. Hums of electricity and morning news voices came through the open window.

"You told me no one but your mother knows about the baby," he said. "Except now I know. And I have already made room for her. You won't have to keep her in that tiny box. Not with me."

She stood and wrapped the robe around her, putting the box in one of its deep pockets. She put her palms on his cheeks, then caressed his neck. He picked her up again as he had last evening in the bright moonlight, raising her nearly to the ceiling. Then he brought her down slowly and hugged tight as her feet touched the floor.

"Tonight then," she said. "Let's have a glass of water."

149

AUTHORS

Glen Armstrong

Glen Armstrong holds an MFA in English from the University of Massachusetts, Amherst and teaches writing at Oakland University in Rochester, Michigan. He also edits a poetry journal called *Cruel Garters*.

Sally Burnette

Sally Burnette is originally from North Carolina, but is currently a double major in Creative Writing and Literature at Eckerd College. Her poetry has appeared in *Poetica Magazine, Bop Deaa City,* the *Eckera Review,* the *Eunoia Review, Deep South Magazine,* and the *London Literary Project.*

Jay Carson

Now a full time writer, Jay Carson taught creative writing, literature, and rhetoric at Robert Morris University, where he was also a faculty advisor to the student literary journal, *Rune.* He has published more than 60 poems in national literary and professional journals, magazines, and anthologies. Jay published a chapbook, "Irish Coffee," with *Coal Hill Review* in the summer of 2012 and a longer book of his poems, "The Cinnamon of Desire," with *Main Street Rag* in the fall of 2012, as well as co-edited with Judith Robinson a collection of Margaret Menamin's poetry, "The Snow Falls Up."

Tobi Cogswell

Tobi Cogswell is a multiple *Pushcart* nominee and a *Best of the Net* nominee. Credits include or are forthcoming in various journals in the US, UK, Sweden and Australia. In 2012 and 2013 she was short-listed for the *Fermoy International Poetry Festival.* Her fifth and latest chapbook is "Lit Up", (*Kindrea Spirit Press*). She is the co-editor of *San Pedro River Review.*

Daniel DiFranco

Daniel DiFranco lives in Philadelphia where he is currently working on an MFA from Arcadia University. He teaches high school music and English. His work has appeared in *Crack the Spine,* and is forthcoming in *Philadelphia Stories* (Winter, 2014). Wanderlust bit him at an early age and he learned the hard way there is no peanut butter in Europe.

Megan Dobkin

Megan spent the last fifteen years as a producer and executive for film and television. After working with writers on such movies as *Girl, Interrupted; Walk The Line; The Recruit; Kate And Leopold; The Vow* and the two middle films of the *Scream* franchise, she began to try her hand at staring at her own damn blinking cursor. She continues to develop projects for and with her husband (writer/director David Dobkin best known for his film Wedding Crashers), while writing fiction, poetry and answering tough questions about science and Star Wars from her two boys in the backseat of her car. In addition to appearing in *Crack the Spine,* her writing has also appeared in *The Bicycle Review, The Eunoia Review, and The Next Family*. She graduated with a degree in English from Kenyon College.

Melanie Faith

Melanie Faith holds an MFA from Queens University of Charlotte, NC. Her writing has been nominated twice for the *Pushcart Prize*. Her poetry chapbook, "Catching the Send-off Train," was published by *Wordrunner eChapbooks* as their summer 2013 selection. She is a writing tutor at a college prep. high school in Pennsylvania and an online creative writing instructor. Her poems, essays, and fiction have been published in the past year at *Vermillion Literary Project, Linden Avenue, Aldrich Press, The New Writer, Foliate Oak, Origami Poems Project, Star 82 Review,* and *Words Dance*.

Janelle Fine

Janelle Fine is a 22-year-old poet and artist from Los Angeles. She found her love for being creative as early as preschool when she began to draw and then started writing poetry in the third grade. She has grown considerably since then, self-publishing her first poetry anthology titled "Wildfibers" at the age of 18. She received her under graduate degree from The Evergreen State College in Olympia Washington. She is currently pursuing an MFA in writing and poetics from Naropa University and is obsessed with matchboxes and miniatures, founding *Matchbook Press* to publish travel size poems and art in matchboxes.

Christina Marie Glessner

Christina Marie Glessner grew up in the heights and valleys of the Pocono Mountains. She received her BA in Creative Writing at Susquehanna University, and she is a fiction MFA candidate at the University of New Mexico, preparing to defend her story manuscript in the spring. She is the current Managing Editor at *Blue Mesa Review*. "In a Ghost City, a Crosswalk Signal Chirps," in *Crack the Spine* Issue 76, was her first publication in poetry.

Matt Hall

Matt Hall has recently finished up graduate work at Monmouth University (English with a concentration in creative writing) and works in New Jersey as a public school teacher and as a college adjunct. He is currently working on his first novel.

Brian Hobbs

Brian Hobbs finds the practice of writing to be the closest prayer to god he can come across. To that extent, he tries to worship with words once a day, even if it is a sentence or a phrase that he scrawls on a napkin in a restaurant and wants to carry in his pocket like everyday gold. He has a Lady of Leaves and a 'Lil bean he loves and spends most of his important time with. He has been published in *Glass: a Journal of Poetry, Red Fez, Crack the Spine, Milk Sugar: a Literary Journal,* and an upcoming issue of *Scissors and Spackle*. He is also a huge fan of Frank Zappa, Doctor Who, and ASMR videos on Youtube.

Tim Kahl

Tim Kahl is the author of "Possessing Yourself" (*CW Books*, 2009) and "The Century of Travel" (*CW Books*, 2012). His work has been published in *Prairie Schooner, Indiana Review, Ninth Letter, Notre Dame Review, The Journal, Parthenon West Review,* and many other journals in the U.S. He appears as Victor Schnickelfritz at the poetry and poetics blog *The Great American Pinup* and the poetry video blog *Linebreak Studios*. He is also editor of *Bala Trickster Press* and *Clade Song*. He is the vice president and events coordinator of *The Sacramento Poetry Center*.

Brianne M. Kohl

Brianne M. Kohl is a fiction writer who resides in Chatham County, North Carolina. Her work has been published in *Black Heart Magazine, Ohio Edit, Crack the Spine Literary Magazine, Corner Club Press, The Bohemyth Literary Journal* and in "In the Hardship and the Hoping: Poems of Northeast Ohio" by *JB Solomon Editions*. She was the best fiction recipient from *Bop Dead City's 2013 Summer Fiction Contest*.

Priscilla Mainardi

Priscilla Mainardi's work appears in *Nurse.com, Pulse Magazine, The Legendary, Crack the Spine,* and *Blood and Thunder*, among others. She holds an MFA degree in creative writing from Rutgers University in Newark, New Jersey, and recently received a grant from Vermont Studio Center to complete her first novel.

Robert Marshall

Robert Marshall's novel "A Separate Reality" was published by *Carroll & Graf* in 2006 and was nominated for a *Lambda Award for Debut Fiction*. His prose and poetry have appeared in *Salon, The Michigan Quarterly Review, Event, DUCTS, Stickman Review, Blue Lake Review, Alembic, Blithe House Quarterly* and numerous other publications. He is the recipient of fellowships from *MacDowell, Yaddo* and the *New York Foundation for the Arts*. A visual artist as well as a writer, his work has been widely exhibited in both Europe and the United States.

David McAleavey

David McAleavey has had work in many journals over many years, ranging from Ron Silliman's mimeo mag *Tottel's* in the early 1970's through *Ploughshares, Poetry* and *The Georgia Review*; since early 2010 he has had over a hundred poems and prose poems accepted/published by *Epoch, Poetry Northwest, Denver Quarterly, Birmingham Poetry Review, diode poetry journal, anderbo.com, FRiGG, Stand, Drunken Boat*, and dozens of others. *Pirene's Fountain* awarded him their Editors' Prize for the best poem in their publication in 2011; in 2012, *Convergence* presented an "Editor's Choice" special feature of his poems; and in 2013, *New Delta Review* has included one of his prose poems in their "best of the web" anthology. His fifth and most recent book is *HUGE HAIKU* (317 pp.,

Chax Press, Tucson, 2005). He teaches literature and creative writing at George Washington University in D.C.

Sean Padraic McCarthy

Sean Padraic McCarthy's stories have been recently published, or are forthcoming in,*Glimmer Train, The Ledge Poetry and Fiction Magazine, The Sewanee Review, Hayden's Ferry Review, The Greensboro Review, Water~Stone Review, Sou'wester, Bluestem, South Dakota Review,* and *The Sand Hill Review* among others. He is four time top 25 finalist in the *Glimmer Train* Fiction open contest, placing second in 2010, and several of his stories have been nominated for the Pushcart Prize. His novel *Where the Birds Go to Die* was recently named a finalist for the Black Lawrence Press Big Moose Prize, and he lives with his wife, children, and a very large Great Pyrenees in Mansfield, Massachusetts. He recently completed work upon a second novel.

Shaun Anthony McMichael

Shaun Anthony McMichael lives with his wife in Seattle. He started the blog *Zine Project Seattle* which features poetry and artwork from street involved youth. He currently works for Seattle Public Schools in a special ed. classroom. His fiction has appeared or is forthcoming in *Scissors and Spackle, Crack the Spine, Litro, Petrichor Machine* and *Avalon Review;* an article he wrote about writing with youth in crisis can be found on PongoTeenWriting.org.

Greg Moglia

Greg Moglia is a veteran of 27 years as Adjunct Professor of Philosophy of Education at N.Y.U. and 37 years as a high school teacher of Physics and Psychology. His poems have been accepted in over 100 journals in the U.S., Canada and England as well as five anthologies. He is five times a winner of an *Allan Ginsberg Poetry Award* sponsored by the Poetry Center at Passaic County Community College. He lives in Huntington, N.Y.

Annelle Neel

Annelle Neel lives in Knoxville, Tennessee. She holds an MA with a Writing Option from the University of Tennessee where she served for 16 years as a writer in development and alumni affairs. She is a member of the *Knoxville Writers Guild, Sisters in Crime*, and *SinC Guppies*. Her work has appeared in *Colere, Hardboiled, Caliban, Forge, The MacGuffin* and *The Storyteller*.

Jos O'Connell

Jos O'Connell is not a normal person; some people would even say that his name isn't even a real name. Is it pronounced 'Joss'? Is it pronounced 'Jose'? Is it pronounced 'Joz'? With a name just as uniquely strange as his work, he wishes that both his work and his name are approached in the same way; pronounced however *you* want. Jos has had verse published in Florida's *Ignition* magazine, as well as, written songs for musicians such as Joe Purdy and C.P. Stelling. He has won awards for his lead-acting, as well as, his writing of the renounced short-film; "Finger In the Fan:" a film based around a young narcissist, directed by up-and-coming film-maker Zac Grigg. Although he has several titles to his name, it is the love for the word and the written language that is truly important to him. He works to create stories that open up the readers eyes without preaching or talking-down. He also works hard to raise questions and poke at boundaries created by the modern stale-state of prose. Joz, or Jose, or Joss, or Jos, is very grateful for you as a reader and hopes that you enjoy his work!

Jeffrey Park

Jeffrey Park's poetry has appeared most recently in *Maa Swiri, Right Hana Pointing, Dark Edifice* and the anthology *Just One More Step*. His digital chapbook, *Inorganic*, is available online from White Knuckle Press. A native of Baltimore, Jeffrey now lives in Munich, Germany, where he works at a private secondary school.

Eliot Parker

Eliot Parker is author of the sports murder mystery novel *Breakdown at Clear River*, a 2012 nominee for Outstanding Fiction by the Appalachian Studies Association. His forthcoming novel, "Making Arrangements," will be published by *Sunstone Press* in October 2014. His short fiction has appeared in *Speck* Literary Journal, *Apex Books, Kentucky Story Press,* and other publications. Eliot is a graduate of the *Bluegrass Writers Studio* at Eastern Kentucky University and currently teaches writing and literature at Mountwest Community and Technical College in Huntington, West Virginia.

Laura Pendell
Laura Pendell has an MFA from Mills College. She grew up in New York City and now lives in the Foothills of the Sierra with her husband and cat. She writes, makes hand bound journals and artists books and tends a garden. Her poems can be found in *Jelly Bucket*, *The Tulane Review*, *Talking River* and *Soundings East* or on line at *Foliate Oak*, *Blue Lake Review*, *Wila Violet*, *Mary: A Journal of New Writing*, *OVS*, *Assisi Journal* and *The Edison LIterary Review*.

Jim Richards
Jim Richards' poems have appeared recently in *Prairie Schooner*, *Poet Lore*, *Comstock Review*, *Texas Review*, and online in *Dead Flowers* and *The Fertile Source*. His work has twice been nominated for a *Pushcart Prize*, and in 2013 he received a fellowship from the *Idaho Commission on the Arts*. He lives in southeast Idaho's Snake River valley.

Marilyn Ringer
Marilyn Ringer resides in Northern California. Her poems have been published in print and online in many journals including: *Nimrod; Drumvoices; The Evansville Review; RiverSedge, Eclipse; Sanskrit; Hawai'i Pacific Review; Poet Lore; Quiddity Literary Journal; poemmemoirstory(PMS); Left Coast; Rea Wheelbarrow; The MacGuffin; River Oak Review; decomP; The Hurricane Review; Eclectica; Slant; The Art of Monhegan Island* (Down East Books 2004). Her chap book, "Island Aubade," was published by *Finishingline Press* in 2012.

Jason Ryberg
Jason Ryberg is the author of seven books of poetry, six screenplays, a few short stories, a box of loose papers that could one day be (loosely) construed as a novel and a couple of angry letters to various magazine and newspaper editors. He lives in Kansas City, Missouri with a rooster named Little Red and a billy goat named Giuseppe. His latest collection of poems is "Down, Down And Away" (co-authored with Joshua Rizer and released by *Spartan Press*, 2012).

156

Carla Sarett

Carla Sarett's short fiction has been published in over twenty five literary and humor magazines—and a memoir about her grandfather appears in the forthcoming edition of *Blue Lyra Review*. Her short story collections include "Nine Romantic Stories" and "Crazy Lovebirds: Five Super-Short Stories," available on Amazon. She is at work on a novel based on the woebegone heroine introduced in "Career Girl" (in the anthology, *Love Hurts!)* and "Skinny Girl" (in *Red Fez*.)

Rochelle Jewel Shapiro

Rochelle Jewel Shapiro's novel, "Miriam the Medium" (*Simon & Schuster*) was nominated for the *Ribelow Award* and her newest novel, "Kaylee's Ghost" (Amazon and Nook) was finalist in the Indie 2013 Awards. She's published essays in the *New York Times (Lives)*, *Newsweek,* and won the Brandon Memorial Award for an essay in *Negative Capability.* Her poetry and short stories have appeared in appeared in many literary magazines such as *The Iowa Review, Stand, Inkwell Magazine, Poet Lore, Compass Rose, Controlled Burn, The Griffin, Lost Angeles Review, The Atlanta Review, Moment.* Her poem, *Second Story Porch,* was nominated for a Pushcart Prize. Shapiro is a psychic who also teaches writing at UCLA Extension.

Michael Dwayne Smith

Michael Dwayne Smith is both post-hippie professor and editor in chief at *Mojave River Press & Review*. His work appears at *burntdistrict, Wora Riot, Stone Highway Review, decomP, Heron Tree, >kill author, Monkeybicycle,* and *The Cortland Review*. He lives near a Mojave Desert ghost town with his wife and rescued animals.

Angela Maria Williams

Angela Maria Williams has been an indie bookseller, workshop leader, editor, and journalist for more than a decade. She is the editor of *Fickle Muses* and holds an M.F.A. from Sarah Lawrence College, as well as a B.A. in English from the University of New Mexico. Her work has appeared, or is forthcoming, in *Tar River Poetry, Poydras Review, Diverse Voices Quarterly, Rose Red Review, Contemporary American Voices, At-Large Magazine, Sage Trail* and *Conceptions Southwest.*

157

Kirby Wright

Kirby Wright was a Visiting Fellow at the 2009 International Writers Conference in Hong Kong, where he represented the Pacific Rim region of Hawaii and lectured in China with Pulitzer winner Gary Snyder. He was also a Visiting Writer at the 2010 Martha's Vineyard Residency in Edgartown, Mass., and the 2011 Artist in Residence at Milkwood International, Czech Republic. He is the author of the companion novels "Punahou Blues" and "Moloka'i Nui Ahina," both set in Hawaii. "The End, My Friend," his futuristic novel, was released in 2013.

This anthology is generously sponsored by Outskirts Press

anything

everything

everywhere

WITH

outskirts press

"It just doesn't get any better than this."
—Deanna O'Leary,
    published Outskirts Press author

Writing Services to help you start, finish, or edit a book.

Publishing Packages to help you publish and distribute.

Marketing Support to help you promote your book.

Visit www.outskirtspress.com for 10% off a publishing package with promotion code: CTS2013

159

Visit www.crackthespine.com to subscribe to our weekly digital magazine or to review our submission guidelines.